A Special Kind of *Twisted*

ONYII UDOH

A Special Kind of Twisted by Onyii Udoh

ISBN 978-1-970072-56-3 (Paperback)
ISBN 978-1-970072-57-0 (Hardback)

This book is written to provide information and motivation to readers. Its purpose is not to render any type of psychological, legal, or professional advice of any kind. The content is the sole opinion and expression of the author, and not necessarily that of the publisher.

Printed in the United States of America.

New Leaf Media, LLC
175 S. 3rd Street, Suite 200
Columbus, OH 43215
www.thenewleafmedia.com

DEDICATION

Richard Udoh my husband. Thanks for loving through my twisted nature and bringing out a more amiable me. Love you lots, Sweetheart.

Acknowledgments

Much thanks to Bola Bello and Edwin Udoh, my longtime friends. Christine Edet, my wonderful editor and friend. This couldn't have come together without their help. I thank them for believing in me and seeing who I really am and for making out time from their busy schedules to read this work. The success is ours; I am appreciative and will forever be grateful.

My love always goes to my heartthrob: my husband. He and the children are God's special blessings in my life. I thank him for understanding, loving and supporting myspecial twisted self. I am deeply indebted to him and the children, without whom I could do but little.

Linda C. Onyeador, its awesome having you as a sister. Thanks for your patience, love and sacrifices. You are the best.

Special thanks to my friends and family, who continue to surround me with love, prayers and support, I cannot list everyone by name, but you know who you are.

To Kelsey Saldana and New Leaf Media team, I say thank you.

I return praise and thanks to the great author of all, God Almighty. Thank you for this special gift of yours and I pray never to trifle with it.

REVIEWS

This is a strong story written with love and detailed attention to the characters. This is something that we are all up against; the will to find peace, the desire to be something more. Very few of us actually have the satisfaction of achieving that.

This novel was an amazing piece of art reflecting that even if you are a little crazy, it doesn't mean that you will not get what you want. If you are twisted enough to try, you will get it.

Rabia Tanveer for Readers' Favorite

'A special kind of twisted' is a reminder of the essence of true friendship, Love and forgiveness. The fact that God's grace is greater than our sufferings, amazing messages that we all can relate to.

I was captivated by the strong and appealing characters in the story and its good sense of humour, got me laughing a few times, which I liked….a lot.

It's a demonstration of what changes can happen with love, care and belief.

Bello B.

This is a refreshing and breathtaking story of ordinary people coping with ordinary life. It is perceptive and shrewd.

Edwin Udoh

This story reaches out and grabs a hold of you. The weirdness of its characters is its strength because they remind us that we could be misunderstood, feel alone and helpless and yet be lovable. The story reminds us that it takes a special kind of strength to love and be kind to people who do not deserve it. And in the end, love conquers all.

Christine Edet

Chapter 1

Zarah sat on the back steps of The Stones Family Restaurant, where she worked. How time had flown, yet she still felt as helpless as ever. Her life had been on a steady decline on the human race ladder. Economically and in every other way, Zarah was at zero level.

On that night, like every other night during her break between the hours of 8pm-9pm, she sat watching the silhouette of homeless street cats scavenging for food.

"Look at them roaming freely, sleeping anywhere without fear. No bills to constantly harass them. They are really better off than I am" she thought.

As she stared, she became consumed as usual, with the anger which had become part of her since she left home. The anger increased in depth with each year that passed. That was the only thing that drove her on. The only yearn in her heart for the future. The anger had become Zarah's twin sister. Zarah constantly reached out to 'her' at the slightest indication of joy in her heart, just to be sure 'she' was there; the remembrance of what she planned to do and must do - murder. Yes, murder.

"Madison, that epitome of all the cartooned wicked stepmothers put in one. How she made me suffer unpardonable hardship for years now without hope of things getting better. I cannot wait to put enough money together to travel back home and do what I must do and end it all." Zarah continued her musing to herself.

She had planned and re-planned this particular murder. She wanted it quick at the same time she wanted it slow. She ultimately wanted to see her suffer, beg for her life. Madison deserved to hear Zarah tell her how she had planned killing her without mercy. She could not seem to arrive at a conclusion on how to end it all. If only she had been able to watch Viola Davis's '*How to get away with murder*' when it showed. She had no one to ask the details of the movie because no one could know what her interests and plans were. Besides, she did not talk to anyone. She only had her demons as companions.

"Oh God, I am tired of all this! Can't I just have a decent life? Just a life where I can pay my bills, afford my meals with ease, laugh again with friends, buy better clothes than these rags I wear and live somewhere better. Just something better, nothing fanciful." She cried to herself exhausted by all the thoughts in her head.

Having lost her mother at the age of five, she became her father's world. Mr. Sam Harrison, a multi –billionaire made sure Zarah lacked nothing. He filled her world; he balanced her life so well that she had no remembrance of her mother. Sam had not remarried until Zarah was seventeen. He had felt she was old enough to be on her own and would soon go off to college. He was not obvious about it but Zarah had known he did not want their world shared with anyone else. So when Madison came into their lives, she could not understand her father's decision and that made her suspect Madison of manipulating her father like the cartooned stepmothers. Her hatred for Madison, 'that half squared faced Russian was clear from the onset. She made Madison realize in all ways possible that she did not need nor want a mother. Madison stayed clear of her, taking little notice of her existence. They coped well, lived separate lives until that unfateful day when the cold hands of death snatched her father away. The memory of that day always set chills down her spine; she had just started her third in Business Accounting/Management. She could never understand how her healthy father, who ate breakfast with her and kissed her goodbye before leaving for Harrison Towers, was said to have dropped dead just like that two hours later in his office. She suspected foul play, she suspected Madison, and Madisons actions afterwards did not help matters. Madison cut her off everything, even when she'd swallowed her pride and went to her for help, Madison had denied her help.

"Can I have a word with you?" Zarah had asked Madison.

"Who, me?"

"Hmm."

"What is it then?" Madison asked nonchalantly.

"I need help."

"Help, what kind of help?

"I want money."

"Money, for what?"

"I have to give you a list before I get money from you?" Zarah had asked sarcastically.

"No you don't, and I don't see why you have to come to me. After all you never wanted nor needed a mother."

"What! I… never mind." Zarah had turned and left.

Oh, how Madison had made her suffer reduced her to less than a rat. She should have known. Russian blood whether half or not remained very wicked. Yet Madison never missed any church service. Zarah had never been a fan of church going, she had never thought much about it. She had gone a few times in the past but not anymore. She could not understand how God allowed someone like Madison come into church, pray to him. Why had he not struck her with thunder or let the grounds open up and swallow her as it had happened in the Bible. No, she did not think there was a God. All the talk was mere fallacy, designed to keep people well behaved and have them come back to church day after day and give offerings. "After all", pastors got to eat, they do not do any form of work," she thought with sarcasm and a bitter laugh.

Zarah groaned as the thought of food reminded her of the pang of hunger in her stomach. She had not eaten since morning except for a cup of coffee a regular costumer had bought for all the restaurant staff at noon to celebrate his pay rise at work. This got her frowning, conscious of time and her surroundings. It was a rude shock to notice a man standing close to the trash dumpsters by her. In his hands were filled trash bags that had tags. At first, she meant to flee right back into The Stones Family Restaurant, fearing an attack, but another quick glance had her noticing the man was well groomed. Zarah stopped, especially as it seemed the man was talking to her. She turned fully to him to hear him say,

"Sorry to startle you, but are you Zee?" he paused, and then continued, 'Zee Harrison? You sure look a lot like her but but...?' His voice trailed off.

Zee, a name she had not heard since she came to Yukon Oklahoma, and one she wished to forget because Zee Harrison no longer existed. Whoever this was, this flash from the past should not be seeing her like this but she was not given to cowardly acts. She would not deny who she used to be, though it awakened many painful memories. She nodded and replied,

"Yeah, I'm Zee ... Zarah Harrison and who are you?"

"I'm Dave, David Duke. Double D of Fame Hostel."

Double D! Oh, how Madison must pay for this, Madison must die!

*** *** ***

David Duke, "Double D," as they called him, graduated top of his class from David Geffen School of Medicine at UCLA. After graduation, he interned at Sparkling Diamond Hospital, about the best in the city of Oklahoma. He was good at his job and loved by everyone. Now, he ran his own practice and planned to open a second clinic. At 33years, he was successful, the toast of most young women in Oklahoma City.

Last Thursday evening, David had got a disgruntled call from his favorite great-uncle, Uncle Leo who was grumbling about how David never came to visit. He eventually cornered David into promising a week end visit to him at his farm on the outskirts of Yukon. He told David to stop by The Stones Family Restaurant on his way and help him pick up their green trash for his pigs, to save him the trip to town. David was quite delighted to help, at least that would save him feeling guilty about devouring the steak he knew he would have for dinner. Steak was usually his great-uncle's specialty and a treat for him.

However, nothing had prepared him for the shock of that Friday night at The Stones Family Restaurant. Having to clear his desk and re-arrange his schedule as he was not going to be in the city for the weekend, he left Oklahoma City late for Yukon. He did not mind, knowing he was going to have a lazy weekend with a lot of pampering from Uncle Leo. Getting to The Stones Family Restaurant, the peace and joy was in no time replaced with angst and apprehension.

He had turned to the back of the restaurant just as Uncle Leo had instructed, to locate the trash bags with his Uncle's name tagged to them. Little did he know that he would be locating more than trash bags. David knew that he was not suddenly having a bad dream but he did not want to believe his eyes.

"That must be Zarah Harrison's look alike." he thought. But no, there was no mistaking Zarah Harrison!

Zee had a distinct face and body. She was a beautiful young woman with class and grace. Looking close, he could still see the beauty despite the dirty haggard look. She looked like she had not been to a salon in recent years. Her usually soft merry dark brown eyes were now black with hostility. With the squaring of her shoulders and the way she carried her head, one would instantly know that she was a woman of some pedigree. Her voice was definitely the same but now laced with something he could not describe. Was it pain, hatred or just plain hopelessness? David could not seem to put his finger on it. 'Who was the woman he just met, where was Zee, what happened to her?' The more he thought about it, the more curious he became. How he wished it was not so late and that he did not have Uncle Leo waiting for him.

He thought he would have got some answers if whatever his name was had not interrupted them. The guy shouted for Zee saying something about her break being over and how she was needed in the kitchen. Wait! Needed in the kitchen? Her break was over? She worked there? At this time? And what about her haggard looks? Whatever happened to her college degree? He was sure she had studied Business Accounting and had graduated. The questions screamed through his mind. Oh Christ! Questions, questions with no answers. He had no idea how he was able to concentrate on his driving. But at last he arrived at the farm and Uncle Leo was ready to fuss over him with stories of the family, questions about his life and his practice and eventually his specialty dinner; steaks.

These took his mind away from Zarah but not for long. Once dinner was over, he excused himself with the pretense that he was tired but his uncle knew better. Uncle Leo knew something was heavy on David's mind, but what could it be all of a sudden? Earlier that evening when he called that he was about to leave the city, and even when he called at Yukon to ask for directions to The Stones Family Restaurant, he had sounded very cheerful and free, not moody and pent up, as he seemed to be at arrival. All his efforts at teasing and questioning him to help draw him out failed. What could be the problem? Uncle Leo sat on his rocking chair by his bedroom window watching the stars. Sensing his nephew's son tossing and turning on his bed in the bedroom next door, his heart went out to him and he said a prayer to God on his behalf, for God to give him sleep this night and to help him find peace in the midst of his troubles. Uncle Leo got up from his rocking chair by his bedroom window, went to his bed, and slept.

David could not help his mood, he felt sorry for being an unpleasant guest despite his uncle's efforts. He barely finished his uncle's favorite treat for him, which was quite unusual, and he could not even remember how it tasted; he just needed to be alone with his thoughts. He took a shower to relax him, and then lay in his bed but could not sleep. He tossed and turned with questions he could not answer. He knew he had to go back to The Stones as it is popularly called around Yukon; he had to find answers to his questions. He had to see Zarah again.

Chapter 2

S teve, Zarah's co-worker in charge of order entries for the day rounded off on his time and was ready to leave. He called out to Zarah so he could hand over to her but she was not there. He went to Tom, who was their supervisor, as well as the restaurant and security manager all rolled in one. Steve told Tom that he was done for the day but had not seen Zarah so he could hand over. Tom knowing where she could be went through the kitchen and headed straight to the back door. He was the only one who knew that Zarah spent her night break times on the steps behind the restaurant. At first, they had all thought that she went out during her night breaks and had all talked and wondered where she went. Then one night, Lemon, the leader of The Emoss, the neighborhood gang, told Tom of the woman that always sat on their back steps between 8pm and 9pm. Tom looked afterwards and confirmed his suspicions. He asked Lemon and his gang to look out for her, that she was under his protection. He considered it fair being that he paid the gang protection money each month. Sure, Zarah was worth adding to his list, even if only because she was an employee of the restaurant.

Zarah was more than an employee; she belonged to the 'household,' to his mind. Strange as Zarah was, the girl who said almost nothing to anyone, always answering in monosyllables when asked any questions. She looked troubled but did not allow any one reach her nor did she ask for help. She never talked about herself even when interrogated. She had looked so polished when she first started, only working the day shifts. But later, she began to look haggard. Even then, there remained a bit of polish. Tom thought of her as being a woman on a vengeance crusade and a stubborn one. For sure, Zarah was strange. They had gossiped, teased and made innuendos at her but that girl never budged. At last, they decided to ignore her as long as she held up her own end of the work, and that she did well. Tom decided to be her guardian angel, always looking out for her, making rules to favor her; stating that leftovers were for the last set of workers and breakfast was free for the first two at work, knowing she was among those who finished last and came in first. That way, he could make sure she got two good meals each day. Zarah was grateful and Tom knew it. The other staff knew too that Tom favored her, so they stayed clear of her, even Jade who hated the very mention of Zarah's name.

As Tom went to open the back door he heard voices and felt an adrenaline rush.

"Is Zarah in trouble? Who is that talking to her? Could she possibly be talking to someone?" All these flashed through Tom's mind in a matter of seconds.

He opened the door to find a fine gentleman with tagged trash bags of the green waste in his hands. That must be old Lee's grandnephew. Old Lee had called earlier telling them that his nephew's son would be helping him pick up the green trash in case they happened to see him doing so. Well he must have been asking Zarah for clarification. As he told Zarah that she was needed in the kitchen, he turned and gave the man an icy look, once over especially when he noticed that Zarah seemed a little rattled by the man's presence or whatever contact he had tried making with her.

As they went in, Tom went to the phone and called up Lemon to find out what he and his gangsters saw, they were always watching Zarah. Lemon told him that the gentleman came for the bags just like Tom saw but probably got fascinated by the statue-like human staring at nothing and wanted to know if it was real or not. This drew laughter from the rest of Lemon's gang in the background and Tom was sorry for asking but felt better though he still watched Zarah closely. She seemed unsettled by that contact and he wondered why. Lemon also told him that the man left immediately he went in with Zarah but Tom's guts told him that that would not be the last time he would be seeing the gentleman.

Zarah could not wait for the restaurant to close for the night at 11pm. She was a bundle of nerves. Back at her place, she found herself taking a cold-water shower despite the weather. She was ready to do anything to steady her nerves. She lay down but couldn't sleep. She was full of agitations. Why on earth did Double D come by when she was sitting out there? Why hadn't he simply picked up what he'd come for and left? Eventually she slept off but it was a sleep full of nightmares. She found herself running from things throughout her sleep. She ran from a giant hand trying to grab her, a huge cloudy figure trying to envelope her, a resounding voice calling her name, the list was endless.

Chapter 3

David woke up to the smell of bacon and toast. He quickly showered and came to the kitchen where his uncle was just putting the coffee on to brew. With one look at him dressed in jeans and t-shirt, Uncle Leo knew the Lord answered his prayer the previous night and gave his nephew's son rest.

"Hi Dave, sleepy head." He called.

"Hi Uncle Leo, I needed the rest. How are you this morning?"

"Good and you?"

"Better…"

"I was hoping we could go fishing this morning. I'd like grilled fish for dinner tonight."

"Oh, wow! That sure would be great; I'm ready whenever you are."

Over breakfast, they talked about the farm business and the general state of things. After they were done, David did the dishes while Uncle Leo went to get ready for their fishing trip. Pulling on his shoes, he offered a little prayer to God to use him reach his nephew's son and help him, because he could still sense the tension within him. They got in the truck and drove down the road to a stream not too far from the house.

"I hope you are better at fishing than I am," Uncle Leo said. "I barely catch enough to make dinner for one."

"Don't worry; with me dinner is a done deal." David laughed as he reassured his Uncle of his ability.

"Well, I have warned you though." he replied.

It was good to hear him laugh his first real and free laugh since he came. They got to the stream, set their rods, took their places and waited. In twenty minutes, Uncle Leo unbelievably felt a tug on his rod. He reeled in the fish and almost got pulled into the water because he was not expecting its size. The fish was about 3.7 pounds. It was a huge surprise to him, because his fish were always about 1.4 – 1.7 pounds. He shouted, "One against you Dave!"

"Shush! You are scaring the fish and you'd better concentrate before that fish pulls you into the water for real," David laughed.

They sat again in silence for about an hour, occasionally glancing at each other and sharing a smile. Both felt a tug on their rods at the same time and burst out laughing as they reeled in the fishes that were about the same size.

"Dinner is finalized and in good time, thanks to you and the luck you brought with you." said Uncle Leo.

"Hey, I'm not the one that caught two fishes of good size. It was you. Thanks to you."

Uncle Leo just smiled. On their way home, they stopped at the diner for a drink and burger. They both ordered iced tea with their burgers. While they were waiting for their orders, David's mind strayed to Zarah once more and that brought a frown to his forehead. His uncle watched in silence. Their order arrived so David took a bite of his burger, and smiled, saying how good the burger tasted. His uncle nodded in agreement and felt it was the right time to reach out to his dear nephew.

"Dave...,"

David turned to him.

"Do you mind sharing what has been on your mind?"

"Hmmm! Nothing. Oh Christ am I that transparent?" he groaned, covering his face with his free hand. "I've been trying hard to be a good guest. 'Well," he continued, "I guess it will help me if I share it. After all, I only have puzzles that cannot fit together."

He went on to tell his uncle about his chance meeting with Zarah Harrison, (his old college acquaintance). How it raised many questions for him without answers. How he felt a need to go back and find out what, why and how come she was at The Stones Family Restaurant and if possible help her in any way he could. At the same time he felt helpless because he did not know where to start, because, the person he saw at the restaurant was different, worlds removed from the Zarah he used to know. His uncle listened without interrupting, knowing that more than curiosity had been aroused in his beloved nephew and knowing he would not realize it.

"Well I think you should give it time Dave." Uncle Leo advised. "Don't be pushy in reaching out to her so as not to lose the chance of knowing what went wrong with her." *Or of knowing that your heart has got involved,* he thought to himself. They finished their burgers and set out for the farm.

At the farm, David set about cleaning the fish and his uncle sat on the rocking chair by the living room window going back and forth. They talked about the weather, recent developments in town and at the little church where Uncle Leo worshipped. He told Dave that they now had a new young unwed pastor that had made all the eligible young women devout churchgoers because they all hoped to get a chance of being chosen as wife. They both laughed hard about that with David wondering how such thoughts had gone through his strict uncle's mind. Nevertheless, he laughed very hard and even asked his uncle for his opinion on whom he thought could be chosen. His uncle responded, "None". That brought some more laughter.

David finished the fish, sauced and put them in the fridge to marinate and they went to freshen up before coming back to prepare dinner which David had declared was his treat since his uncle said he brought the luck.

At dinner, David told his uncle that he would be leaving right after church service in the morning instead of his earlier plan of driving to work on Monday morning from the farm. He told his uncle that some emergencies came up. Uncle Leo knew Zarah Harrison was the emergency; he did not mind but wondered if she was worth it. He prayed again, for God's guidance and for David to triumph through God in this emergency.

They went for the seven a.m. service the next morning, Sunday. David sat absent minded throughout the service. He sat planning the week ahead, calculating how to reschedule his appointments in order to have at least a two hour break one day so he could drive the 46 minutes back and forth Oklahoma –Yukon to check out Zarah Harrison. He knew the earlier the better, so he could get over with it and concentrate on other things. Therefore, he chose Tuesday, and mentally rescheduled his appointments, hoping to remember the changes just right for Chloe, his secretary to note. When his mind strayed back to church he sat appraising the young pastor and the young women and true to his uncle's words, there were quite a number of them sitting mostly up front. The young pastor was actually handsome in a wholesome way; no wonder the mad rush by the women. As for the women, he chose to vote with his uncle, thinking it would be wise of the pastor if he overlooked the chase or at least played it out for as long as he could hoping it would make real devout Christians out of these women. He chuckled at the thought of the drama that would soon be unfolding in this little countryside church. At his chuckle, Uncle Leo glanced over at him and smiled, sensing his thoughts about their young pastor and the women. After the service, he drove Uncle Leo home, said his goodbyes and started his thought filled drive back to Oklahoma City.

Chapter 4

Madison just got off the phone with Paul, the private investigator she had hired two and half years ago to find Zarah. The news had always been the same month after month, no headway. She had even hired a second investigator on a short term contract to investigate the first to be sure he was actually working. Sure enough, Paul was truly working on finding Zarah. Nevertheless the story had remained same for two and a half years. Slowly depleting her funds and causing her untold sorrow. Zarah Harrison! "God, why?" She was an enigma when she was home with her and beyond words even a greater enigma in her absence. "How did she get herself into this?" Why had she not married an ordinary man with an ordinary child? Why had she let herself fall in love with Sam Harrison? Why had she let herself be talked into believing that it would work out between her and Zarah? Why did she not walk away from the onset as Zarah made her stance with her clear?" These were her constant daily questions. She only knew that she had loved, still loved Sam Harrison. She loves Zarah. Who would not love the beautiful, free spirited and well-adjusted young lady Zarah had been before the death of her father that seemed to have cast a dark shadow on her, even leading to her disappearance till date. Zarah's ill manners only showed up with Madison, she vehemently refused to have anything to do with her. She called her Miss Madison like a stranger. Zarah refused all manner of communication with her or help from her. Once, Madison had helped to pick her book that had fallen on the floor but Zarah told her to put it back on the floor, that she had hands of her own. Nevertheless, she loved her as her child because of her commitment and love for Sam and God. Imagine her shock when Zarah came asking for her help. Unfortunately her shock did not allow her respond rightly to Zarah. She secretly feared that she had actually needed help then. Zarah, not one to beg, never came back to her and she stupidly did not reach out to her, more out of fear than pride.

To Madison, that was her greatest undoing, because that had widened the gap between them and then Zarah left. But why would Zarah come to ask her for help if not to mock her? She had it all, Harrison Towers as a whole. It was all hers but she never touched it and now she had gone missing.

She had a bad feeling about this; she knew that the law had secretly investigated her when she reported Zarah missing, which was why she hired her own private investigator. Zarah was indeed an enigma, whether absent or present. How could such a sweet child cause so much painful drama with her presence and worse with her absence? Zarah! She had to find her before anyone else. She must put an end to this; even if it was her only accomplishment. She must know for herself that Zarah is alive and what went wrong.

Madison was convinced Zarah lived, she could feel it and strangely, she could feel her. She never envisaged this part of her life when she met and married

Sam. They had met ten years ago under very unusual circumstances; she had not known who Sam was. They struck up a friendship that lasted for two years evolving into love before Sam proposed. Sam waited for her to say yes before telling her who he really was.

*** *** ***

Sam Harrison, a multi- billionaire was a handsome man in his late fifties but still had his youthful looks. He had lost his wife Michelle in a ghastly car accident one evening as she was returning from a charity fund-raising event. A moving truck ran into her on the freeway. Sam could not understand and forget it. Zarah was only five, how is he able to raise her alone? But alone he decided to raise her, not letting her out of his sight, not letting her want anything. Zarah became his world and he, hers.

He had met Michelle six years before at his friend's wedding where she was one of the bridesmaids. It was love at first sight. He could not take his eyes off Michelle throughout the entire ceremony. During the reception, when it was time to dance, he saw his opportunity to make contact.

"May I have this dance?" Sam asked.

"It's about time we break the ice so you can stop staring at me and causing people to talk." Michelle surprisingly responded.

This warmed Sam's heart, knowing that Michelle had noticed him too and liked him...he believed. It made it easy for him to talk to her and without mincing words he told her that he liked her and wanted to date her, but Michelle just replied with "let's see how it goes."

They chatted like old friends and found out they had a lot in common. Sam left the wedding wondering and curious about Michelle's earlier reply. At the time, he could not care less; all he cared about was her friendship which he had secured. 'We will truly see how it goes,' he had chuckled to himself.

They dated for seven months. Sam was in love with Michelle and knew he wanted more than friendship from her; he wanted her as a wife, mother of his children, life partner and companion. But he was afraid, afraid that she might not want him and afraid that she might want to wait for later. He feared losing her, knowing that the relationship would turn awkward if she rejected his proposal. This was a huge burden to him for some time. Then one night, late in the seventh month of their relationship, they had attended a wedding anniversary dinner of one of Michelle's friends. There was so much romance in the air, mounting pressure on Sam. Unable to endure any longer, he took Michelle to a corner and popped the long dreaded question. Michelle flew into his arms singing "Yes!" She asked what took him so long. They were married a fortnight later.

Sam was a wealthy young man; he had inherited his father's cosmetic company. Michelle was working as Assistant Manager at one of the city banks. She resigned from her job because Sam said she was better off managing him and their home. He did not want to share her or her time with any employer. Michelle found she could get busy in other ways without formally working. She became involved in a lot of community service and mission work. Sam did not mind since he got to go with her to most events.

They had Zarah in the second year. It was a trying period for them both. From non-stop vomiting from the second week of the pregnancy, to non-receding swollen feet, acute back and joint aches, pregnancy induced high blood pressure, headaches, and spotting. Michelle had to be on mandatory bed rest four months before her due date. Sam decided he hated pregnancy; he almost lost Michelle during the delivery. He swore Michelle would never go through that again. He could not bear the thought of another ordeal. He got a vasectomy when Zarah was two months old without prior discussion with Michelle.

Michelle could not believe the resolute nature of the man she married. She loved him dearly and could not imagine life without him, but knowing how deeply he loved her was another feeling she could not explain. Zarah became the center of their lives, knowing without discussion that they would not be having another child. She still took part in community and mission work as time permitted until that 'unfateful' night. She had gone to a fundraising for the refurbishing of the orphanage in the Inglewood district area. She had planned to go with Sam but he called late that afternoon to say he would be running late as some business partners came into town and wanted him to have dinner with them. He contemplated cancelling; after all they had not notified him in good time. But Michelle would have none of that; she insisted that he should go to dinner with them. The Bridge Company had been good longtime business partners of Harrison

Inc., so she guessed that entitled them to ask Sam to dinner without a prior appointment.

Sam gave in to Michelle's reasoning and went to dinner with their partners from The Bridge Company. Until he died, that was Sam's only regret in life. Michelle went to the fundraising held at Inglewood. It was a huge success; they raised over and above the estimated amount. On her way back, along the Santa Monica Freeway, she had a head on collision with the drunk driver of a red GMC Yukon. The impact sent her black Z4 BMW flying. It somersaulted twice in the air and landed with its left side. The driver of the red Yukon died instantly of tachycardia and had a deep gash right under his left shoulder blade. She was air lifted to hospital with a broken left arm, a broken right leg and two broken ribs that punctured her lungs. Sam came as soon as he could to the hospital accompanied by Mathew Bridge, founder and owner of The Bridge Company and his son, Joel.

Michelle saw Sam through the tubes and machines she was hooked onto, smiled at him and mouthed "I love you", and that was it. With a smile on her face and her right hand in Sam's, she was gone forever. Sam was broken, hurting to the point of going into shock. He was admitted and he stayed the night for monitoring. He regretted seeing that day, the fundraising, the dinner, everything. He tried taking consolation in seeing her at her final moment and thinking she seemed to have waited for him before giving up her last breath. But he couldn't, he was sick to the depth of his stomach, felt lost and alone. Sam shut himself away from the world for over a month, until some business decisions that demanded his attention could not wait any longer.

He cut off from all social functions. The only ones he attended were the ones involving Zarah, mostly school activities. He was a ghost of himself. His friends worried about him but after almost four years, he started socializing again much to his friends and business partners' delight.

Women in his circle had got tired of flirting with and teasing him. They had given up with the conclusion that something had gone wrong with his libido. On one occasion, Sam Harrison ran into Carol, a close friend from his college days. They had reconnected a few months after Michelle's death, when Sam was still in the blues. He couldn't even remember what their conversations were about. Carol, still unmarried and very good looking with great figure, became a constant caller. He knew she was flirting with him, saw all the signs but refused to acknowledge them. When he couldn't bear it any longer he deliberately cut off every form of contact with her. Carol's ego was hurt but she just felt she would give it time and meeting Sam again after such a long time felt to her like a sign and a chance. She could not lose it.

"Hi Sammy, long time." Carol said, with her brightest smile and eyes sparkling with pleasure.

"Hi Carol, good to see you and you really look good as usual." Sam replied.

"Thanks, I'm glad you noticed. So what brought you out here? Don't tell me you are on a date?" Carol quipped.

"I'm meeting some friends for drinks." Sam said, smiling.

"Hmmm... Good to know that you now socialize again. Shall we meet up for dinner and catch up?" Carol asked with an upturned face and an alluring drawl, batting her lashes and flirting with him.

'Sure..., that will be great! Sam said, trying to sound lured in.

'Say... Wednesday night?" Carol asked.

'No, Friday night will be better, if that's okay with you?" Sam responded.

"Sure, come pick me up at seven, dinner is on me." Carol said, with some pride.

"Wow! 'Can't wait!" And with a raised eye brow, Sam said good bye.

Carol winked with her left eye and blew him a kiss, thinking she at last had another chance to nail Mr. Sam Harrison.

Carol couldn't imagine her luck. Friday night, full of possibilities! She had to make sure to end up in Sam's bed... "By God, the guy is not a monk, it's time someone rid him of his celibacy." She murmured to herself.

Sam met up with his friends but remained a little distracted and amused. He could see right through Carol and knew it was a dangerous game he played, especially since Carol showed no resentment at the way he had cut her off in the past. But, a game it was and he felt up to it.

Sam was at Carol's at seven on the dot Friday night. Carol was ready, dressed in a black satin evening gown with a plunging neckline that showed off her deep cleavage and full chest. The dress enhanced her narrow waist and lushly rounded pelvis, her skin glittered like it was polished to a delicate high shine. Sam reckoned that it had been a long time since he took notice of a woman in this way and he liked the awareness it gave him.

They went to one of the expensive restaurants in Santa Monica; the food was rich and the wine delicious. The conversation was full of questions from Carol about Sam's life and a lot of innuendos on how she wanted the night to end. At first Sam was excited and curious at the idea of having Carol in bed in some hotel for the night. He definitely had no plans to take her to his bed, he still considered that his space with Michelle. Carol was all smiles and laughed at everything Sam said, she found many excuses to touch him, winking and batting her lashes at him. She literally made clear what she wanted from him. He enjoyed the attention given, though a little amused with it. Dinner over, they left for a nearby club. Carol wanted to dance in hopes to set the mood for what she expected to come. They arrived to a slow song playing and Carol was elated saying that was her favorite.

As they danced, Carol clung to him as if her life depended on him. She fixated on him. The scene was so absurd that other couples on the dance floor moved a little bit away and glancing knowingly at them. It was more than he could handle, it became repulsive to him, the excitement of the early night died. He preferred to do the chasing, he preferred intelligent conversations, he preferred light play and laughter together; he liked his women beautiful with attractive features but he did not like seductive women and he definitely did not like Carol. She seemed to have nothing in mind except getting into bed with him. And after they slept together, what's next? This was indeed a dangerous game and he recognized it for what it was. Carol must have had a plan but he was sorry, he wasn't ready to be part of it. This time he intended to maintain his distance from Carol. As the music ended, he more or less tore Carol from himself with Carol protesting for more dances as he led her from the dance floor. Away from the dance floor, he explained that he had an early morning flight to catch but Carol said the night was still very young. Sam agreed but maintained that he still had to go, because he had some work to finish up before bedtime.

They left, but on their way to Carol's house; she seemed not to mind her hand wandering and marveled at Sam's indifference.

The man must be made of steel or the death of his wife must have literally killed him, she thought. Sam saw her to her doorstep and said good night, refused the coffee she offered. He was one foot down Carol's front stairs when he heard,

"At least a good night kiss and a hug is in order."

Sam knew that was trouble; he took a deep breath and braced himself for it. Turning he meet Carol smiling with deadly mischief dancing in her eyes. He tilted her head up and bent his for a quick kiss but Carol wrapped her arms around him and clung to him. Sam firmly unclasped her arms and set them by her side with a firm goodbye. Carols eyes shot daggers at him,

"Brute," she muttered, opened her door and slammed it before Sam could reach the last step.

"Don't let the door hit you." Sam whispered, smiling to himself.

He was elated by the feelings Carol stirred up, it had been a long time he felt that way, and boy the woman was good at what she evidently knew how to do. He had assumed he might not be able to be with another woman but while it was not to be Carol, at least he knew he was ready for a female companion.

Sam dated other women but nothing lasted. Most turned out to be like Carol, beautiful, desperate to get into his bed, no intelligent conversations, some very possessive but all of them to his thinking had one game plan, to be 'Mrs. Harrison'. Sam was at loss as to what he was looking for. He knew he was not looking for a Michelle but hoped to find a woman who could catch his attention and keep it. He picked up the attitude of chatting up any attractive woman he met. He found himself betting before each encounter that there would be no difference. It amused him to estimate how long it would be before each new woman began to fawn and flirt. But then, nine years after Michelle's death, he met Madison.

He had missed his 1:30pm flight from Atlanta to Los Angeles due to a delayed meeting with a new business partner, so Sam had found himself rushing into the airport at 3:10pm determined to catch the 4:00pm flight. As he got to the counter, he found business class was no longer available so he got an economy ticket, his mind fixed on getting back home to Zarah. Wondering when last he sat in the economy section of a plane and how he was going to make it through the four and half hour flight, he walked into the airport lounge and noticed a lady to his far left settling into a seat. There was something striking about her slightly square face and brownish blonde hair in a ponytail. He thought of wagering to himself that she was just like others but something told him this one was different. His excitement grew, he walked with the assured confidence of a man confident of securing his target. At fifty-seven Sam Harrison was handsome, full of health, bold and a sight to behold and he knew it. He intended to put all these to use to charm this lady and while away the time even as a 30 minute delay of the flight was announced. Sam walked up to his target and enquired if the seat next to her was taken and she said no without looking at him. He sat down and said hello. Madison answered with a half way glance at him. She was typing on her iPad and Sam concluded she must be chatting with her boyfriend or some sort. Minutes later Madison closed her iPad and heaved a sigh.

Sam glanced at her and said "Hectic day?"

"You can say that again," she replied. "I have virtually been on my feet since I woke up this morning."

"Doing what, if I may ask?" Sam said with a raised left eyebrow.

"Oh, meetings, presentations, I work as a marketing manager of 'Dream It,' an architectural company. I came to make a presentation to a potential client down here. It went well though; I just got off chatting with my boss. You know, keeping him up to date with the whole thing."

"So, you live in California?"

"Why? Yes, Bakersfield. Why?" she asked, surprised at the switch in their conversation.

"Really? I have got a friend down there in Seven Oaks. Where in Bakersfield are you?"

"Rio Bravo."

"Rio Bravo, hmm. I have played golf at the golf course there several times. By the way, I'm Sam, Sam Harrison."

"Madison Drew."

"So tell me Madison how is life in Rio Bravo, you seem to like what you do, huh?"

"Yes actually, I like the part that I get to move around. I'm not the office kind of person you know. The pay is good, and so are the bonuses for every client I bring in. The job goes with superb accommodation, a car and insurance. It's just great for me."

"You make it sound like all you have to do is feed yourself."

"Yes really." She laughed.

"You like that someone else takes the pains for every other thing about you. Is that not like being an item on the list of what the company has to do?"

"Maybe, but you know what, I don't care."

"Oh... I'm sorry, someone is touchy this evening."

"My apologies, I didn't mean to sound off like that. It is just that all my life more or less I have been pushing and pulling all ends of my life, so it is feeling like heaven to have someone else take some of the load off my back, you know."

"Hmm. I see..."

"No, you don't. Don't get me wrong. You see, I kind of saw myself through college. My parents died in a car accident in my freshman year. I was seventeen."

An ice dart shot through Sam's heart at the mention of car accident.

"I was left with no relations." She continued. "My Dad, a Russian, had severed all form of contact with his people a long time before then and my mom's all-American family never supported their marriage. I worked my ass off going through college and lived in all manner of accommodations. It was hell, save for the college insurance my dad had taken out sometime before and his life insurance. It taught me hard work though. So you see this feels like a little pampering. I know it totally means that the company owns me. Yes I don't mind but I am not a fool. I am saving and planning. Did I tell you that the money is good?" Madison said laughing.

"Yes, you did and I can see it's really good".

"I like this girl already," Sam thought. On the flight to Los Angeles, Sam swapped with Madison's seatmate so he could sit beside her. They talked about life in Bakersfield, talked more about her job, politics and so on. Obamacare was a hot debate for them. Madison was fully in support pointing out clearly that a lot of people with her background didn't put themselves there, they just happened to find themselves there and she believed they had right to any help they could get especially with healthcare. Sam was careful with the topic, he didn't really express his views, and he only led her on to talk. He sensed its importance to her.

When they landed, Sam offered her dinner and she accepted. They went to a nearby restaurant and ate dinner, talked some more and exchanged contacts. She gave Sam her card but Sam just took her phone, typed and saved his unlisted direct line in her phone. They parted with Sam promising to send good clients her way.

Sam knew he had to see her again. There was something attractive beyond that slight pink complexion, an almost square face, jet black eyes, jet-black hair like velvet and her openness. He liked the idea of having a conversation with a female that wasn't hitting on him. Maybe it was because she doesn't know him 'Sam Harrison'. Whatever, He didn't care and he loved her company. On the drive home, he was already planning a visit to Bakersfield. Later, just before he retired for bed he called her.

"Hi, this is Sam, you remember?"

"Oh hi, sure I remember, I don't forget easily." They laughed.

"Okay, I just wanted to know you got home alright."

"I did, thanks for asking and thanks again for dinner."

"Oh, you are welcome and I really did enjoy your company."

"I did too."

"Good to know I still have got the charm."

"Yeah, you do."(Giggling)

"Can we meet up, let's say this Saturday?"

"Are you asking me out?"

"Well, actually yes, I will come to Bakersfield."

"Okay, that sounds good to me."

"Great, Saturday it is then, have a great night."
"You too, oh... hello. Are you there?"
"Yes."
"What time do I expect you?"
"Noon."
"Okay, goodnight."
"Goodnight".

Sam spent the next two years shuttling between Santa Monica and Bakersfield. He loved every moment of it, except for the lies he had to tell. He never told Madison who he really was because he feared she would only want him for his money. After six months of meeting Madison, he bought an estate management firm 'Better Homes' and told Madison he worked there as a manager. He proposed to Madison in their eighteenth month and when Madison said yes, he asked her to take two weeks to consider the fact that she would have to leave her job, secure life, Bakersfield and move to Santa Monica where she would have think of house rent, phone bills, insurance and the like. Madison still said yes after two of the longest weeks in her life. Sam didn't call and refused to take her calls. She was torn apart wondering if she had imagined the whole thing. Sam on the other hand didn't have it any easier, he kept away to give her space to really think and to give himself space to think and calm his nerves. He knew the time had come to tell her the truth of who he really was. Madison still said yes after the two weeks and then it was time to tell the truth. He told Madison about Zarah and that he was the owner of Harrison Inc. and Better Homes. Shocked, Madison accused him of lying and called their relationship fake.

She called off their relationship and for the next four months, Sam begged and pleaded, using everything he had to persuade Madison to forgive him and marry him. He would send dozens of flowers a day from one of the local flower shops in Bakersfield until Madison went and told them to stop making deliveries to her. Sam started using other flower shops randomly from all over the states. He went crazy. Sometimes at the mere thought of her, he ordered a flower not minding how many he had sent already. Madison wrote him and told him to stop. He answered and told her that as soon as she started taking his calls, answering his e-mails and agreed to marry him, he would reduce the flowers but not stop entirely. Eventually Madison relented and they got married. Sam gave Madison "Better Homes" as a wedding gift.

Zarah, didn't like the idea. She couldn't believe her father had a relationship for two years and she hadn't known. She called Madison a gold digger. Sam tried assuring her that Madison was far from that but she refused to accept it. Sam would have given anything to see the two women he loved on earth become friends. He admired Madison's efforts to maintain peace in the house despite Zarah's outbursts of rudeness. He never knew Zarah could be rude and hateful until Madison came into their lives. He had a talk with Zarah, assured her of his love for her and demanded respect for Madison. He asked that she refrain from her hateful comments, confrontations and innuendos to his wife.

Zarah wept uncontrollably that night, Sam had never spoken sternly to her before.

Chapter 5

David woke up on Tuesday with so much excitement and trepidation. Chloe was wonderful. She arranged his day so he could have two solid hours free instead of the one hour he had asked for, so he could spend some quality time with Zarah and still return to work in good time., He felt great, although anxious, he couldn't wait. At last he would have some answers. Getting to the office, he realized Mrs. Benson was on the list for office visits. He smiled knowing his day wouldn't be dull or hectic at all. As a general practitioner, he had many patients like Mrs. Benson who made office visits part of their routine out of boredom rather than because they were truly ill.

Mrs. Benson, a widow in her eighties, would use most of her time to talk about her children, how many times they had called or not called her in the week, the weather, her grocery shopping and to hassle David about marrying and having kids early. David indulged her throughout her visits, smiling all the way with little questions here and there. She said David reminded her of her son, Michael who had died in the line of duty in Iraq at thirty-five leaving behind a wife and three kids.

Today, David enjoyed Mrs. Benson's office visit as usual but his mind was on his visit to Yukon. The thought of seeing Zarah again in that restaurant made him anxious. Mrs. Benson noticed and teased him.

"How was your weekend David?"

"Great, Mrs. Benson and you?"

"As usual, but I can't help wondering what has your mind occupied. Have you found a girl?" She winked.

David's heart jumped at the irony of the questions but he just smiled and said he would tell her whenever he found one. The morning went well and he had time for a quick drive to the post office to mail some pictures to his parents who still preferred hard copies of anything. On his way to Yukon he kept wondering how he was going to explain his coming to Yukon and how he was going to ask Zarah to lunch. He rehearsed and rephrased his questions and Zarah's likely questions a zillion times before getting to Yukon. He got to The Stones Family Restaurant at 12:58pm on the dot. He parked at a parking lot a little distance from the entrance, telling himself that he needed the walk to soothe his nerves. On entering the restaurant, he glanced around and judged the restaurant as being only two steps removed from a diner., He walked to a table, sat and waited, thinking it best to ask for Zarah from any waiter that approached him and at the same time give himself the time and space to observe things. Zarah approached him within two minutes with a menu and her order chart poised to take his order. On recognizing him, she stiffened and with clenched teeth, she asked him what he would like to have.

"I will like to have lunch with you," was his response.

"I'm sorry I can't, I'm working. So, what can I get for you?"

"I thought you are due for break by one."

"I can't remember you asking. I am waiting to take your order."

"Honestly, I don't want anything, just to have lunch with you."

"Very well then, enjoy your time."

She moved to clear another table two spaces away. David sat staring at her. For a moment there he had thought he was in luck having her be the one to approach him but here she was at what was supposedly break time and she was so cold. He thought back to their first encounter the other night and compared it with this encounter. He reflected that then, she had been a little open, surprised maybe but this …? She didn't even acknowledge knowing him. How strange. The Zarah he knew was not like this. Gone with his train of thoughts, he didn't notice Tom approach his table and take the seat opposite him. He startled when Tom said 'Hi.'

"Hi." David responded

"Having trouble with the waitress?"

"Zarah?No, not at all."

"Oh...! You know her?"

"Yes, I do."

"I didn't see you making any orders then?"

"And what does it matter to you?"

"Well, I'm Tom, the manager of this restaurant. So I consider it my business especially seeing Zarah so stiff and pink all over on seeing you and talking to you."

"I'm sorry, I didn't mean any trouble. I thought I could have lunch with her, we were schoolmates and I consider her a friend. But, we lost touch after my graduation and I just happened to run into her last weekend when I came to pick up your green waste for my uncle, old Leo as you guys call him."

"I see. So, you are old Leo's beloved nephew. Well, as you can see, Zarah is busy."

"Does she ever go on break?"

"She does, at 12 noon." David raised his left eyebrow and Tom felt inclined to explain.

"You see Zarah is her own person, she doesn't really like company so she takes her break earlier and that works for everyone. As you can see she is here at break time when most staff are off, which is good and she is one of our best hands."

"Doesn't like company?' Shaking his head, David said, 'this is not the Zarah I know. She used to be lively and enjoyed people."

"Tell me more."

David smiled. "There is nothing to tell."

"So then, can we get you something on the menu?"

"No please, my appetite is gone; I wish I could speak with her."

"Not today man, come back tomorrow or any other day before 12 noon, maybe you will be in luck." Tom said getting up from his seat.

"Yeah, I guess so. I'm David by the way."

"David. Nice meeting you."

"I should be leaving; I will see what I can work out. I might as well have some coffee; I think I will need that."

"So you can sit and look at her some more?"

David just stared at Tom without a word and Tom nodded.

"I will serve you."

When Tom brought the coffee to David, he told him to stare less at Zarah, that he was making her jittery. David ignored him, took his coffee and stared out of the window. His mind was empty for a while as he sipped his coffee. He finished his coffee, paid for it, took one last look at Zarah, smiled to Tom's hawk like watching eyes, nodded and headed out of the restaurant.

Tom turned into his office to answer the ceaselessly ringing desk phone and guessing who it could be, he bellowed a "Yeeaah."

"Is your phone for fancy?' yelled Lemon from the other end.

"No, as you can tell."

"That guy from the other night causing any trouble?"

"No, he is cool."

"So, what the hell kept you from coming to the phone?"

"I was entertaining him," Tom chuckled.

"You what?Must be kidding."

"I'm not, he is cool I say."

"Is he still there?"

"You should know better, you are the area surveillance."

"So what did he come for?"

"He thinks he knows Zarah."

"He what? He must be nuts."

"No, he is not, I think it's true."

"Zarah knows him?"

"Yet to find out but, it doesn't look otherwise."

"Sounds like a good story is brewing over there, Keep me posted. Just got told that your cool guy zoomed off looking like the door hit him." Lemon laughed with the others in the background.

"Yeah, he feels and looks terrible. Lemon, I will keep you posted, thanks for looking out for us."

"Any time man!Will come over for a roast this weekend."

"On the house. Will be expecting you."

Tom sat back in his office chair, staring at the phone and wondering what sort of story Zarah was hiding. Was she a college graduate? Coming out of his office, he found her at the counter, noticed others had returned from their lunch break and there was still a small tide of customers, thankfully.

"Hi Zarah, in my office please."

"Oh, in a minute," Zarah replied.

"Now." Tom insisted.

As Zarah stepped into Tom's office, Tom asked her to close the door behind her while he sat staring at her.

"I know you didn't call me to your office just to stare at me?"

"No, I didn't."

"Soo..?"

"You tell me.'

"Tell you what?" Zarah said irritated.

"What I need to know."

"There is nothing that you don't already know."

"Damn it! Zarah, don't play smart with me."

"Smart? Hmm..., please Tom be a little direct with your questions."

"Ok, now you are dumb." Zarah's eyes narrowed and turned jet black in intensity.

"Ok, for starters," Tom continued, "who is that young man that scared the shit out of you?"

"Nobody that matters."

"Nobody that matters? But, you were so rattled by encountering him that one could hear your teeth chattering?"

Thinking Tom must have an impressive sense of humour, she smiled inwardly and answered:

"You know that often happens when you see someone you haven't seen in ages and you are not expecting to see the person."

"He said he knows you, that you guys were college mates." Tom spoke through clenched teeth, irked by her offhanded attitude.

"Oh! You guys talked, huh?"

"I take that to mean that what he said is true."

"Look Tom, I prefer not to talk about this."

"I can see that, but I need to know that you are not in any sort of trouble and that guy is speaking the truth."

"You don't have to worry, Dave is harmless. It is just wrong timing."

"Dave... huh? Tell me Zarah, what are you fighting?"

"Drop it Tom!" She snapped. "Can I get back to work?"

"Yes, you can. I hope you know you haven't seen the last of him?"

"I will deal with it then."

"Oh yes you will, oh yes you will."

As Zarah left, Tom couldn't help wondering at the emergence of this Zarah. He had never seen or heard her speak this way and he realized he had never had any discussion with her that was not related to work. Even those were always short and in the midst of other people.

Zarah left Tom's office feeling betrayed but not knowing by whom. Where did Dave surface from? Why did he care that she was here? Who was she kidding? Of course he would care or at least be curious and knowing Dave, he would not give up until the he learned all he wanted to know. But why was she jittery as if she was guilty of something? She was guilty all right, but not until the act was done. Being guilty of intending a crime was for religious people, which she clearly wasn't. This was a distraction she didn't need, she thought, shaking her head to clear it. Getting to the counter, all eyes turned to her, probably wondering why Tom had called her to his office with such urgency. Yes, they should wonder. It was tactless of Tom to have summoned her like that but he was not totally to blame. The guy himself had to be scared shitless at having someone surface here looking for her. She smiled at the thought of Tom being scared and realized that it had been a very long time since she had been amused over anything. Pushing the thought aside, she continued from where she left off.

Jade quietly left for Tom's office not knowing that Zarah saw her sneaking away. Jade met Tom still deep in thought.

"Hi."

"Jade..."

"Yeah, what's up?"

"Where?"

"Any problems with Zarah?"

"And you will be happy to hear the details?"

"Not that I care."

"Then go back to your work."

"I'm just curious; will you blame me for asking?"

"Jade, there is no problem whatsoever okay!"

"Sooo.., why did you call her?"

Taking a deep breath Tom replied:

"It's personal!"

"Oh..., personal? I knew it! You have been harboring some feelings for Zarah, that black hearted bitch. That's why you treat her so differently."

"You must be crazy, Jade."

"Eh.., I am crazy I know, just deny it." A broad menacing smile on her face.

"Jade please, I have got a lot on my mind. Just go back to your duty post."

"Yeah, yeah I will. But I want to know what is happening around me".

"Jade, if you don't go back to work this minute I will remove an hour's pay from your paycheck."

"Yeah right, you will," Jade turned to leave, pausing at Tom's next words.

"And please keep those hideous thoughts to yourself."

"Asshole!"

"You are welcome." Shaking his head, Tom picked up his desk phone to call Greenie Store for the delivery of some orders he had made two days ago.

Jade went back to her work at the serving area; on sighting Zarah, her eyes blazed with envy, enmity and annoyance. Zarah just looked past her, unperturbed and reaffirmed her decision to stay out of Jade's way at all times. Jade didn't know what infuriated her more. The fact that she didn't know what was happening or the way Zarah seemed unaffected by her obvious enmity. Steve, Max, Kate and others where watching. As soon as Zarah left to attend to some customers, Steve stepped to Jade and asked what she learned knowing she must have gone to find out why Tom summoned Zarah. Jade just muttered: 'that son of a bitch wouldn't say anything." Steve recognizing her mood quickly went back to his post.

***   ***   ***

David felt more confused than before coming to The Stones Family Restaurant, his heart was heavy with disappointment and something more. The excitement of the day had been crushed and on top of that more mystery had come up than he cared to solve. What must have gone wrong with Zarah? How he wished to be with Uncle Leo, at least to have someone to talk to, to have his uncle soothe his nerves with a listening ear and calming words.

"He is not far from here you know'?" He heard his heart telling him. "And you know you are always welcome at the farm."

He kept driving to Oklahoma City lost in his thoughts and it seemed like from nowhere he heard police sirens behind him and saw the vehicle's light flashing at him, signaling that he should move over.

Shocked, he looked at his speedometer "Shit, that is much." he muttered. What was happening to him? Over speeding and swearing? He pulled over on the shoulder, parked his car then waited with hands resting on top of the steering wheel. They came up to him, asked where he was coming from and where he was going. They took his driver's license and checked it, asked him what he did for a living, whether he had been drinking, if he was on any drug of any kind and a couple of other questions. The cops asked him to step out of his car; they searched his car, carried out an alcohol test on him and finally asked him if he knew he was speeding. When he replied that he hadn't known he was speeding, they asked where his mind was. He just realized that in the bid to ignore his mind's urging to go down to uncle Leo's, he had over stepped on his gas. Apologizing, he told the cops that he had had a disappointing lunch and probably took it out on the car. The cops looked at each other, talked aside and turned to him, handed back his driver's license with a warning to drive more carefully, and he drove the remaining distance to the clinic disheartened.

*** *** ***

Zarah felt relieved, her morning shift had ended by 3:30pm as usual. She quickly changed into a day dress, took her purse and left the restaurant. She felt bad for not having her normal afternoon bath and siesta which had become a religion for her every afternoon once she got off work but, she needed the air and space and they equally needed that in the restaurant especially Jade, she thought to herself.

Immediately outside the restaurant, her mind went to David. "Why Dave, why?" kept echoing in her head. Dave shouldn't have bothered with why she was here. It seemed so wrong that he tried to find out. It was going to spoil everything. They are going to know about her at the restaurant. Tom was already curious. Thinking about it, he might even try reaching out to her father, friends or even Madison. Madison! The thought brought the taste of bile to her tongue. Yuck! she spat.

'Yo, yo, yo.., who do we have out? The mouse is out to play at last?' Hearing the sneer a few steps to her left, she looked up; she saw a tall Caucasian guy with one front tooth missing and a scar under his right jaw. The guy was leering at her leaning against the wall with some other guys. She smiled at them and said hello, determined not to show her anger at his disrespect and fear at their presence. She kept walking.

"Yo, you not stopping for a chat, mouse?" The guy snarled back.

"Let up Spot!" She heard another guy snap back at the man with a missing tooth.

She noticed that the guy who snapped back looked better dressed, and in authority. Maybe he was their leader. Who knew and who cared. She had things to sort out in her head.

On getting to the thrift store down the road she turned in, and walked from one row to the other admiring dresses, shoes, tops and so on. Suddenly a feeling of pity and regret overcame her and she nearly burst into tears. She quickly made her way to the bathroom, splashed some water over her face, dabbed it dry and chided herself for indulging in frivolous thinking. She didn't know which was worse. The thought that she couldn't afford to buy any of the things she had admired or the fact that she was actually in a thrift shop, admiring things and feeling sorry for herself. Sighing sadly to herself, she left the bathroom and walked out of the shop. She had to keep her mind on what mattered.

Once outside, her mind went back to Dave. She had to make an effort to talk to him; at least put his mind at rest so he didn't go digging up things that were better left the way they were. Nobody needed to know where she was. Maybe she would tell him about her father and how she lost everything. 'That sounds like a good enough reason to keep him away,' she thought. Raising her head, she saw that the group of men was still leaning against a wall in her path back to the restaurant. She had never noticed them all the while she had walked this street to and from work while she was lived in her own apartment. Maybe they were new to the area, she thought. Taking, her time, she studied them from beneath lowered lids. They were not badly dressed for gang members, if that was what they were. They looked like they could have guns. Guns! Her body seemed to come alive with a feeling she could not describe but she knew she would befriend them.

As she passed them, she deliberately turned and looked at them. Resting her eyes on the man who seemed like their leader, she nodded acknowledgement to him and smiled. Lemon nodded back without a smile, Spot snarled, Jamie, Janet and others just looked on with hawk like eyes. She could feel their eyes boring holes in her back. She was happy they had taken notice of her. It was good she took this walk and even better if she made it regular so she could get familiar with the gang.

Chapter 6

As she went into the restaurant, she met Tom standing hands in his pocket, mostly hidden from customers by the shelf right before his office door. One look at his stern face and Zarah regretted coming through the front door. She should have just come in through the back door or at least not have looked toward the shelf. But that was out of habit. Behind the shelf was Tom's duty post, standing back there gave him a view of all the activities in the restaurant, with its semi-open layout. Unless one looked closely, he couldn't be seen. So, they had got used to glancing for that figure behind the shelf. Having less than forty minutes before her night shift started at 7:00pm, Zarah moved right past everyone into the store where she slept to change into her work clothes and freshen up.

The night shift went well. With Jade gone there was less tension, even a little playfulness. She retired for the day feeling a little light headed though she couldn't put her hand on the reason. She took a shower and lying down instantly slept off. However, she found herself waking up at intervals in a pool of her own sweat. The nightmares had returned and this time more scary; the giant hand grabbing her but surprisingly, gently caressing her, the huge shadow enveloping her like an enclosed wall which made her screams literally bounce off like a resounding voice echoing her name.

She would wake up in a panic drenched in her sweat, only to go back to sleep and go through the same nightmares. It was a tiring night but she survived it waking earlier than usual ready to face the new day. She looked forward to work, anything that would get her mind of the nightmares hanging heavily over her like a dark cloud.

*** *** ***

David met Denise, his Filipino girlfriend waiting for him in the waiting lounge. He had not called or taken her calls since last Friday before he left for Uncle Leo's. One look at her face and tense posture told him the rest of the day wouldn't be easy.

"Hi Denise!" He called out.

"Hi stranger..."

"Yeah right, come on in to the office."

"Hmm."

She followed him into his office and sat opposite him glaring at him. He took his time in removing his coat, emptying his pocket and checking his mail basket. He finally sat down, looked at Denise and asked if she had had lunch, to which she replied that she was not hungry.

"Okay, so how are you?"

"Very well, thank you and you?"

"I'm good, thanks for asking."

He clasped and unclasped his hands for three whole minutes while Denise just glared at him without saying a word. He knew she was not going to let him off easy and though he knew he owed her some sort of explanation or apology, he did not feel up to it. David had come to understand that she was more in love with the idea of dating a successful doctor than she was in love with him as a person. They had been dating for two years now after a purely circumstantial start. When they had been introduced at the house warming party of one of David's patients, who also happened to be Denise's senior colleague, Denise had taken to him at once. She was easy to talk to, intelligent and very friendly. David found himself calling her often and having lunch with her and in a span of three months their relationship changed. They became a couple and it didn't take long for David to notice that Denise was very selfish and needy. She said she loved him but she really loved the fact that he was a doctor with his own practice. She never showed interest in anything beyond whether he called her or not, where they went to lunch or dinner or how often she could come to his place. She liked that he could afford the coolest restaurants, luxury presents and frequent shopping. She had never asked about his parents or shown an interest beyond what he tells her of them. Whenever he asked about her parents, she answered with a wave of her hand saying "they are fine", and would quickly move on to another conversation. Once, he had insisted on knowing more and confronted her. Her reply was that there was nothing to know and it was not as if they were getting married tomorrow.

Clearing his throat David said; "Well I'm sorry I missed your calls."

"Hmm."

"And I didn't call or return your calls."

"You were that busy?"

"Not really, just happen to have a lot going on right now."

"Uncle Leo? Is he alright?"

"He's fine." Like you care, he thought.

"So what took you back to Yukon?"

"Some stuff that came up."

"Some stuff?"

"Yeah, you know, over the weekend as I was there with Uncle Leo, some stuff came up and I'm still trying to work it out.'"

"You are not going to tell me, are you?"

"No, I'm sorry. I don't even have the whole story yet, just bits and pieces."

"And this stuff is that big that it can overshadow me? You didn't call while you were down there over the weekend. You didn't call when you came back. You refused to take my calls or call back."

"I'm sorry..."

"Today is Tuesday, you know? Friday to Tuesday, that's five days."

"I'm sorry."

"You see I don't care what you do but don't ignore me. You could have at least told me you wouldn't be available so I could plan other things for myself."

That's it, David thought, not that she cares. She won't even persist to know what stuff he was dealing with. She was only concerned about her inconveniences. How he had been with Denise for two years now was suddenly a mystery to him. She was so shallow and self-obsessed. What did she really want out of this relationship? No, the question should be, what is he doing in this relationship? …at this point he heard Denise saying;

"I can see you are really occupied with this stuff you are dealing with and I honestly don't feel I should be burdened with it, so give me a call when you are done with it."

"What do you mean?"

"I mean I'm going away for some time and I hope you will be done with whatever it is you are piecing together by the time I'm back."

"Going away to where and for how long?"

"I'm thinking of Hawaii for two weeks."

"What about work?"

"It is still work, I'm writing a documentary on vacationing in Hawaii."

"Okay, but I thought you didn't do field work anymore."

'Yeah, I changed my mind. I feel I need some time away by myself. I can't be around a guy who seems to be more interested in "stuff."'

"Yeah right... I can understand."

"That's all you can say?"

"What am I supposed to say, can I change your mind?"

"No!"

"There it is. Enjoy yourself."

Smiling scornfully Denise said goodbye and stormed off. David practically collapsed in his chair. He couldn't believe his luck. Two weeks! "Two weeks of no distractions, which give me enough time to sort Zarah's mystery," he chuckled with a bright smile on his face.

He reached for the intercom and called for Chloe to come in. He told her he was ready for the rest of the day, instructed her to reschedule his time on Thursday so he could be off between 11:30am to 1:30pm. Chloe pointed out that he was supposed to have a meeting with their new would be client "Echoes", a company that wanted to take out a retainer with them. Silent in thought for a moment, he asked her to give them a call and request the possibility of meeting earlier or later. He could feel a surge of renewed energy to pursue the mystery around Zarah, thanks to Denise and her impromptu field work. He called Uncle Leo and told him he would be coming down on Friday evening for the weekend. He asked Uncle Leo if he should help him pick up green waste at The Stones but Uncle Leo said no, that he had worked out an arrangement with a local who went into town everyday but he was glad that David would come to visit without being cornered into it. He asked about his clinic, his health, the weather in the city and Zarah. David told Leo that Zarah was part of the reason he was coming down to Yukon at the weekend. Uncle Leo smiled, but was surprised when David asked him why he was smiling. He told David he knew he had not seen the last of that girl. David found himself shouting, "No! No! That's not how it is." He even stood up to lay emphasis on his denial. Uncle Leo told him not to worry about explanations but David insisted he would explain everything at the weekend.

Chloe walked in to announce his next patient and to inform him that the Echoes were willing to move their meeting to 9:30am on Thursday. She explained the problem with that was how it clashed with Mr. Clifford's office visit. They stared at each other for some time and both burst into laughter simultaneously. With a wave of the hand and still laughing David told Chloe to send in the next patient and think up something to be done about Mr. Clifford. He asked her to confirm the time with Echoes. Still laughing, Chloe shook her head and left to send the next patient in. The next patient was a woman in her late thirties. She came in with severe pains in her lower abdomen. After all the necessary examinations David sensed a need to refer her to a gynecologist so he wrote down some tests and a prescription for pain medicine. He asked her to come in on Thursday hoping to get her test results before then. Then he remembered Thursday was already begging for time but this could be an emergency. It will stand, he thought, others will be sorted out but this is an emergency, this woman is in pain. It might well be an infection, so the sooner the better. Chloe was going to have his head but well, "a man's gotta do what a man's gotta do." The rest of the day went well until Chloe came in to update him on Thursday's appointments.

"Dr. D. I can't believe you asked Miss Dew to see you on Thursday when you are aware of how unreasonably tight Thursday already is."

"Yes, I know Chloe, please calm down."

"How will I calm down? I have been at my wits end trying to figure it all out and you are here compounding it.'

"I will have you watch your words."

"I'm sorry, but honestly, I am beside myself."

"Did you give her a time?"

"No, I told her I will call her tomorrow before 9:00am."

"Good, now let's see..., what time did you give Mr. Clifford?"

"I gave him 2:00pm."

"Have you notified him of the changes?"

"No"

"Good. Very good. Now I will see the Echoes by 9:30am, which I will try to wrap in 30 minutes so by 10:30am I should be back to see the two patients for 10:30am and 11:00am. Leave for Yukon at 11:30am or there about, be back before 1:30pm.' Seeing the look on Chloe's face, he emphasized; 'I will make sure of that so as to see our 1:30pm. Have Miss Dew come in at 2:00pm and Mr. Clifford at 2:10pm. Others can follow as previously scheduled."

"Can you use only 10minutes for Miss Dew?"

'Yes. I only have to review her test results and write prescriptions or referrals, and please take the 10minutes out of Mr. Clifford's time. You know we normally give him 45minutes, so on this Thursday he will make do with 35minutes."

"Are you sure that will be enough?"

"You know, he only pays for 30minutes, and I grant the extra fifteen minutes just because of his age. I bet you he will not know the difference, I will make sure of that."

"How, when coming out here is one of his treasured moments?"

"Let's see how it goes, I can promise him a home visit, you never can tell." David said with a wink at Chloe.

"Yes you can, you little devil,' Chloe said laughing. 'Only God knows what those old folks see in you. Well it's time to go. I will make the changes and have them ready for tomorrow morning and afterwards I will be on my way."

"Okay then, thanks for putting up with me. You are the best." David said to her with his sweetest smile.

Chloe was a middle-aged divorcee with two grown children. She was a trained nurse administrator but doubled as his secretary. Chloe's efficiency in running the clinic with the other staff was one of the things David cherished about her.

David tidied up, packed his things and left for home satisfied with the day and full of hope for tomorrow.

Chapter 7

Madison sat cross legged on her favorite chair by the window overlooking the lake. The last update from Paul on her laps unfolded. She had read and re-read the letter and still couldn't bring herself to accept what Paul was saying. How could he terminate their contract after two years? His profile had said he had no case unsolved. And to think that she had invested two solid years of misery and spending without limit, though he offered to pay back twenty percent of the money she had paid so far. But how would that give her the peace of knowing what had happened to Zarah? Paul had disappointed her, had left her with no alternative than to fight for her peace. The peace and freedom to live her life again no matter what anyone thought. So far Donald & Associates had handled the affairs of Harrison Inc. She was sure they thought she was rich because of the gratuity she received on Sam's death and the increase in her monthly allowance. She needed to finalize matters. She couldn't continue like this. Better Homes had become solely hers when Sam died but she had sold three quarters of it to buy a new house. Selling Better Homes took her off from active participation in the company's matters. The boredom of just sitting around had begun to get to her and she had equally become tired of waiting and looking forward to pay checks.

That was a life she had left behind and she hated its reoccurrence. She had to get back to an active life. Sighing, she was forced to accept Paul's decision, forced to agree he was right on point. Maybe she had been a coward not to have accepted the hand writing on the wall all along but now she was being pushed to make a decision, thanks to Paul.

With a sad smile she lifted the letter, folded it with care and put it back into the envelope then dropping it on her laps, she patted it as if to comfort it. She knew her intended action might trigger fresh investigations concerning her, but she couldn't care anymore. Her life had to go on. She had to go find her copy of Sam's will and read it again, covering every line especially the conditions therein before calling on Donald & Associates.

Standing up slowly still with a sad smile on her face, she went to the chest of drawers against the wall by her writing desk and opened the second drawer. Reaching inside, she pressed the invisible knob of same colour as the wood finishing that opened to reveal an enclosed safe. Her smile broadened, the secrecy of this safe gave her joy and some sort of power. She brought out a big yellow envelope labeled Harrison, pulled out the contents onto the table and sat down. Half way through the papers she got up, took the papers to her copier and made copies of them. Getting back to the table she placed the originals back into the yellow envelope and put it back into the safe with the letter from Paul. Locking the safe and closing the drawer after rearranging the little assortments inside, she sat back on the chair and started going through the papers again with a strange look on her face. She knew she was looking for something but she couldn't remember what it was. Telling herself to relax, that she would recognize it when she saw it, she got a neon lemon highlighter poised to mark it when she found it. Moments later, she found it, marked it with the highlighter, put the highlighter away, took an envelope like the one from the safe and put the papers in it. Putting it down on the table she patted it.

Smiling more broadly than usual, she told herself that she needed a little pampering before going to see her lawyer. Putting the envelope into one of the drawers of the table she got up, went into her room, gathered her purse and car keys and left for the salon. Her favorite salon was near Redondo Beach, and driving there, her mind went to her life with Sam. When she met Sam it was like having sunshine after a cloudy long holiday. Sam was a breath of fresh air. Despite their age difference they connected well. She knew they were in love and wasn't surprised when Sam proposed. Imagine her shock when he told her who he really was. Her anger wasn't the truth he kept from her; she could understand that in a way. She was angry at herself for being too silly in love not to have read in-between the lines. There she was all of a sudden with a multi billionaire on one hand and a girl ten years her junior to mother. She should have run as fast as her legs could carry her then and never look back but she was too immersed in love to care. Now her life was muddled up. She was a widow with a possible murder on her hands if not two murders, if the law decided to investigate the death of Sam. What a mess! Well she had given it time, four years of alienating herself from all that concerned Sam and Zarah. She'd moved out of Sam's house, bought a smaller house for herself and bought a car. She wanted no part of what was not given to her, wanted to be free from Zarah. She had been alone, away from everything, only seeing her cleaner and gardener twice each week. But it was time to take back her life, time to start again.

Speaking of taking back her life, what would she do with the house? Sam's house as she chose to call it despite the fact that Sam willed it to her on the condition that she remains a Harrison. She had hired a cleaning agency to maintain the house and they were being overseen by Donald & Associates. Well, she would sort that out tomorrow when she visited Donald &Associates. For now, she was headed to indulge herself. Barbara was at hand to attend to her at the salon. They exchanged the pleasantries of longtime friends. Barbara went to work, fussing over her, washing, trimming and flat ironing her hair. She applied all manner of treatments, saying Madison's hair lacked nourishment. Madison encouraged her as she enjoyed the scalp massages. Her hair done, Barbara started with her hands and feet. The massage from the pedicure and manicure reminded Madison of what she had missed and she truly enjoyed it. She waxed her legs and plucked her brows, eventually leaving the salon feeling like a million bucks.

First thing after breakfast the next morning she called Bill, Attorney At Law and requested for Bill in person. She spoke to him and scheduled a meeting for 10:00am. Coming off the phone with Bill, she called up Donald & Associates and scheduled a meeting for 12noon. She dressed up wearing a peach colored sheer blouse with little flared sleeves paired with mixed print palazzo pants and mint green pumps. Her purse picked up one of the subtle colors of the mixed print palazzo pants. Her jet black velvet-like hair was brushed to a high glossy sheen and bounce, and swept to right. Her face was lightly made up in nude colors. She knew she looked gorgeous. She walked into Bills office and Bill's jaws dropped. Bill had taken care of partial sale of Better Homes, as she hadn't wanted to use Donald & Associates.

Bill, a flirt who mixed business with pleasure, had made advances to Madison in the past but she had rebuffed him. Today, he found it difficult to concentrate on the matter at hand, Madison had caught him off guard. As Madison brought a copy of Sam's will and asked that he review its terms and conditions and advise her before she went to meet with Donald and Associates. Reviewing Sam's will and pointing out some necessary matters and her scoring points was not a problem for Bill but it wasn't the matter uppermost in his mind. He found he still wanted this woman, she was very attractive and today she really killed it. And that got Bill thinking. Why would she go to this length to look good for a simple meeting with him and later Donald and Associates? She looked dressed to kill and very distracting. And why did she want analyses of the terms and conditions of her husband's will, outlining her authority to possess all? Something smelled fishy. Perhaps she was not as innocent as assumed. He suggested he could make a copy of the will for himself for a more detailed review but Madison declined. He asked to call on her sometime later, Madison told him with a disarming smile that her stand remained same. She thanked him for his time though she had paid for it and walked away while Bill gazed after her lustfully but still perplexed. Madison stopped at a caféfor a cappuccino, digest what Bill had told her, think and compose her nerves and thoughts before her noon meeting with Donald and Associates.

Done with her cappuccino, she went into the restroom, freshened up and left for her noon meeting. She knew she was going to have her way, she could feel it. It had been a long time she felt this way, confident and sure of herself. She missed it and right now it meant everything to her. Nothing would take it back, she told herself. Yes, she knew that questions would arise, even a possible investigation into Sam's death and Zarah's disappearance, but she couldn't worry about that now. Maybe this was what she should have done all along, and maybe it would have forced the law to find Zarah, save her the fortune she wasted on Paul and the three years of her life she had wallowed in fear, regret and uncertainty.

Seated in the conference room of Donald & Associates with their top management, Christy the head of the firm was saying that before Madison could take over the affairs of Harrison Inc. she would have to meet the conditions as stated in Sam's will and move back into Sam's house. Madison objected, asking her to go over the Will's terms and conditions again carefully. She pointed out that living in the house was only a condition if she wanted to maintain the house as hers whereas taking over the affairs of Harrison Inc. was her responsibility if Zarah was incapable. There was a brief silence while everyone averted their eyes except Madison. She had taken them unawares. When she called to schedule a meeting they had thought she wanted to negotiate for more money. None of them had envisioned her asking for a complete takeover of Harrison Inc. And her style! They had all noticed the reemergence of the old Madison, although a little different. This Madison seemed a whole lot more resolute with no care for the world. Christy didn't like it; she didn't deal well with fellow women who were confident and aloof, taking no notice of her authority and personality. With men, it was always different. She hadn't yet met a man who did not notice her. Christy could not let Madison get away with this; she couldn't walk in here and just make demands and expect everyone to fall in line. Mrs. Harrison or not, she had to follow her call.

Recovering from her silence, she told Madison that she would look into it and give her a call back. But Madison had come prepared, not ready to be pushed around. She had always sensed that Christy didn't like her, so she had just one resolve; to reach a conclusion that afternoon. So she spoke up.

"Christy, as much as I'd like you to take your time, I would like to see the current state of affairs with Harrison Inc. I'd like to see the accounts."

Christy told her it could take the whole day to which Madison responded that she did not mind spending the day with them. This infuriated Christy and pushed to her limit, she could see her subordinates were enjoying her discomfiture.

She flared up at Madison, "You know you can't just walk in here demanding for every other thing to stand still."

"I can and I will." Madison retorted.

"Oh no, you can't. I am done with you." She sprang out of her seat.

"No you are not, you show me what I want to see or I will sue you for breach of contract and mismanagement."

"What? What an affront?"

"Affront? No, no, nothing like that." Madison said with her sweetest smile, still sitting down. "You see the contract states that you are to give us a quarterly report which you have never done and we can demand an update at any time, hence the retainership Harrisons Inc. has been paying."

Christy pulled her unbuttoned jacket closed and buttoned it. She sat down, cleared her throat and with a controlled voice she told Adam, the head accountant to see to Madison's need then she turned and asked Madison if there was any other thing they could do for her.

"Oh yes, I will not just want to be talked through it. I will want a print out of the financial statement for the last four years and I want to initiate the process of taking over the affairs of Harrison Inc."

"The print outs, you can have them right after Adam finishes with you. As for the process, I believe scheduling another meeting is in order."

"Well, I will see you in your office as soon as I finish with Adam. Thanks for having me." Madison stood up to leave. Making her way to the door, she looked back and saw that all others at the table were on their feet tidying their things to go but Christy sat watching her with her eyes shooting daggers. As their eyes met, Madison smiled knowing that the battle line had been drawn and she believed it could speed things up. She was in a haste to get her life back.

Madison was satisfied with the accounts statements Adam showed her but would want another accountant to verify them. She noticed that right from the month of reading Sam's will, the percentage of net profits that had been for Zarah remained untouched, even at the time she had come to her for money years back. She wondered why, so she asked Adam.

Adam explained that Zarah wasn't supposed to have access to the funds until she had finished her professional exams as an accountant. Madison asked where Zarah was supposed to be getting funding from if she wasn't allowed to access her account.

"Oh actually, Zarah was not and is not left without funds for the time being, Better Homes pays a certain amount into her account every month for her up keep." Adam replied.

Better Homes! Madison almost fainted, turning pale and her lips quivered. No wonder Zarah had come to her for money. But how was she supposed to know? Why had Sam kept this from her? Had he feared she would have refused, if told?

"So why wasn't this read to me? When I was taking over Better Homes?"

"It wasn't read to Zarah either because it wasn't in the will. Sam only mentioned it because we had asked him the same question on how Zarah would be funded till she could have access to her account."

"I guess he felt it inconsequential."

"Perhaps. Are you alright Mrs. Harrison? You look drained all of a sudden."

"I am fine, just wondering what more I will be discovering."

"Hmm."

"Well Adam, thanks for your time. I deeply appreciate it." She took the printed financial statements and left for Christy's office.

With a resigned look, Christy waved her to one of the seats in front of her as she entered her office. Madison sat down and thanked Christy.

"I hope you are satisfied with the financial reports?"

"Oh yes, I must say I'm impressed and I commend you."

"Fine, thanks. So what else can I do for you?"

"Mm, I talked about taking over the running ofHarrison Inc., so how soon can I start?"

"Yes on that, we will need to notify the board to schedule a meeting for proper handing over and to welcome you on board."

"And how soon can that be done?"

"I will go online right now and send them an e-mail then I'll let you know their decision as soon as I get a reply."

"Please do and make it an emergency."

"Sure. I will copy you in the e-mail. Will there be anything else?"

"No, that will be all till I get their reply."

"Well it has been nice having you over after such a long time."

"Yeah, it feels good to be back to activity once again and thanks for making out time for me." She ignored the sarcasm she thought she heard lacing Christy's farewell words, rose from her seat with her eyes fixed on Christy and extended her hand for a hand shake. Christy rose and took her hand, responding that Madison was welcome anytime.

Madison left for home with a feeling of accomplishment. She was already mentally sorting through her wardrobe. After almost four years of fruitless spending and hibernating, she felt it was time to reassess and update her wardrobe. She would have to go through everything, discard whatever didn't fit the 'Now Madison' and go shopping. She needed power clothing, clothes that made statements without words. Getting those should keep her occupied until her take over.

Chapter 8

Waking up Thursday morning was exciting for David. He didn't need his alarm or Chuzzy, his bulldog fussing and barking over him. He was excited to start the day. He was rolling with his appointments for the day by 8:30am. Less than an hour later, he left for his meeting with the Echoes. The meeting went well and he agreed to have his lawyer go over later to sign the retainership contract. He was back to the clinic before 10:30am, ready for next patients. Unfortunately his 11:00am patient cancelled due to some travel emergencies. Having enough time on his hands to spare, he decided to go down to the Vet's to make the weekend boarding appointment for Chuzzy and by 11:30am he was on his way to Yukon filled with so much anticipation. He got to The Stones Family Restaurant just in time before Zarah's lunch break. He met her at the door as she was leaving.

"Hi Zarah, just in time for lunch!"

"David! Hello, were you waiting for here for me or what?"

"No, I just pulled up."

"Coming from where?"

"Oklahoma city."

"Right and you are here for more green waste? Don't you think it's too early?"

Laughing. "No. I'm here to for a chance to have lunch with you, yes?"

"Ermm, I don't know. I would prefer to take a walk."

"As you like, walk it is then."

"Oh no, I can't deny you your lunch. You go right on with it and I will just take a walk all by myself."

"Zarah?"

"I'm sorry Dave, I actually would like to walk alone."

"Since when did you like solitude?"

"Since life left me alone in this world."

"Zee. Please don't shut me out. I really want to talk with you. Let's have lunch and talk. You need a friend, I know and I'm here."

"There is nothing to talk about."

"Fine, don't talk if you do not want to talk but let's have lunch together for old times'sake." After staring at David for some seconds she said okay.

"So, do you have anywhere in mind?"

"You tell me, you are the one that drove down here wanting lunch."

"Fine, at least I can ask you to go back to your restaurant."

"You better not."

"Typical of Zarah to put one on the spot," he thought, chuckling. He told her of a restaurant he saw three blocks away. But she started grumbling that she was not dressed for such a place. David obliged and opted for another location not so far. He ordered a burger with iced tea and she ordered a chocolate muffin with a yogurt grateful she had said yes to this lunch. The arrival of their orders broke the ice for them as they sat watching each other. Taking a bite of their lunch, they complimented the food and David took the opportunity to ask her how long she had been living in Yukon.

"Four years now."

"Four years! That's a pretty long time."

"What about you, how long have you been in Oklahoma City?"

"Seven years."

"Which hospital do you work in? I can remember you studied medicine."

"I run my own clinic."

"Wow! That's great. I know you are a very determined young man. This is really great. And how is the clinic doing?"

"Great, I thank God."

Nodding, Zarah remained silent with the shadow of a sad smile on her face.

"What about you, how are you doing?"

"Fine." She said with a distant look on her face.

"Do you like it here in Yukon?"

"Comme ci commeça"

"What of your job do you like what you do?"

"That's all I can get."

"Hmm," David stared at her, thinking to drop that line of conversation and to give it time so as not to push her away.

"How is your father?" He asked instead.

"He is dead." she said as cold as stone.

"Dead? When?"

'Six years now."

"Oh I'm so sorry, that would be just as I graduated?"

"Yep"

"What about your step mother, what's her name again?"

Zarah stiffened at the thought of Madison. David, sensing the tension in her at his question, reached out a hand and patted hers saying it was okay if she didn't feel like answering. But it didn't stop him from wondering why she should stiffen up at the mention of her step mom. As usual he thought to give it time. Glancing at his watch and seeing it was almost 1:00pm, he realized he didn't have more time right then. Zarah glanced at hers as well and smiled.

"My break is almost over. I need to be on my way back to the restaurant."

"Sure, and I need to be on my way back to the city to meet up with my 1:30pm patient."

"Well, thanks for lunch. It's made a difference in my stereotyped afternoon."

"You are welcome. Say I see you for dinner tomorrow?"

"I don't have that luxury. I will be working."

"Why, you can't take out time?"

"No."

"Okay, but why? At least give me a reason."

"Do I have to?"

"At least I will understand how it is you work all day. Zarah, you must realize I have questions. Why would Zarah Harrison be working as a waitress for four years now? Come on Zee help me out here, I am going crazy with curiosity, talk to me."

"Yeah, so you satisfy your curiosity and then you are gone."

"Gone? To where? Come on Zarah give me some credit. We were good friends that just lost contact and for me nothing has changed. I'm so happy to be reconnected to you. Please do not push me away."

Zarah, taking a deep breath said, "My morning shift is my regular job and the night shift is in exchange for board."

"Board! Where?"

"In the restaurant," Zarah said waiting and watching for his reaction. But when David who was already prepared for the worst showed none, she continued.

"I sleep in the restaurant store."

"The store! How big is that?"

"Well, big enough that I got a corner."

"That's callous of them! Couldn't they have given you the money or even rented somewhere for you?"

"No, please do not call them names. I wanted it that way. I more or less forced them into it out of desperation."

"Huh? Zee, you seem to have a lot to tell. Look, you should have a weekend off, let's talk."

"And that will happen how? You think being friends in the past means you can just walk into my life and order me about at will?"

"No and yes. I don't have the right but I can't keep on going crazy with questions about what happened to you and what you are up to. So my dear Zee, I will be picking you at 6:00pm tomorrow Friday and you are returning to work Monday morning."

"And I'm supposed to just pack up and follow you?"

"Yes."

"You must be crazy." She reached for the passenger's side door. Opening it and stepping out, she told David to stay out of her business that she didn't wish to see him again.

David nodded and told her he was sorry but she had just made her business his business. "See you on Friday at six" he called out as he drove off.

Zarah was infuriated. How dare he? How dare David think he could just walk into her life and give her orders? Maybe he had forgotten nobody ordered Zarah Harrison around. He needed a reminder come tomorrow. She walked into the restaurant, red in the face with anger.

On seeing her face, her colleagues steered clear of her. Tom, standing at his usual post, smiled to himself. He had been told about David taking her out and he found himself thinking he liked the outcome, he had never seen Zarah this ruffled. This was a good sign, it showed she was human, and he smiled again.

***   ***   ***

David was furious with Zarah as he drove back to the clinic. Why was that girl so independent, so head strong and bent only to her will? Something was so wrong somewhere with her and she didn't seem to care. How was that possible? Why had she grown so cold? Zarah Harrison living in a restaurant store? Crazy strange, that's what it was. What happened to Zarah Harrison? Was she mentally ill? No, he didn't think so, but she could be suffering from depression caused by her father's death. But that did not explain why the only daughter of Sam Harrison, supposed heir to Harrison Inc. would be working as a waitress and living in a store. So many things did not add up and Zarah better be prepared to talk come tomorrow.

Chloe informed him that the 1:30pm appointment canceled and he just mumbled; "Great, just what I need." Chloe didn't know whether to take that to mean 'great that's good' or 'great, what a bad day.' She meant to ask him but decided against it. He didn't even stop to ask why. David sat on his chair behind his desk with his head thrown back, squeezing his eyes shut as if to squeeze out the memory of the late morning from his mind. He silently cajoled himself to think of a strategy to get Zarah to join him tomorrow. He was determined to use his unexpectedly free 30minute to come up with a solution for tomorrow with Zarah. Within a minute of focusing his mind, a thought came to him. He reached for his wallet, pulled out a card and picked up his phone. On the second ring Tom on the other end picked up the line.

David identified himself and told Tom he needed a favor from him.

"If it's something I can do." Tom replied.

"Yes, it is what you can do. It is about Zarah."

"What about her?" David could sense the protective warning in Tom's voice and wondered if it was a good idea to seek his help but decided to go ahead. The worst he could do was refuse and the sooner the better so he could move on to his next plan. He told Tom what he had learned that afternoon and asked if it was true, which Tom said yes to.

"So why did you agree to such a thing?"

"She baffled everyone when she came asking for the night shift in exchange for boarding. Zarah gets paid for her morning shift and exchanges night shift wages for a sleeping space. At first, when we told her it was not possible, she turned pale, looking ready to faint. There was panic in her eyes as she begged saying she had no other place or means because her property agent had kicked her out due to none payment of three months'rent. She offered no other explanation when questioned further and refused when we offered to pay the rents. Mr. Stone Jr. could not say no to her, she is about our best staff, never taken a sick day off, extremely polite, never been late to work and carries out her duties well. She refused all kinds of help. Maybe she was afraid she would default again and get kicked out again."

"Fine. I understand you but I think there is more to what is happening to her."

"Like?"

"I don't know and I need to find out."

"So how do I come in?"

"You see, I can't find that out in an hour, even if I have lunch with her for the next two weeks."

'So?'

"I want to take her away for the weekend, I'd like to pick her on Friday by six and she will return on Monday morning."

"Then tell her. How does that involve me?"

"She doesn't want to hear of it."

"So let her be."

"No! I mean you don't understand. Zarah needs help more than she can admit to herself. I am willing to pay for her time so that you can get another person to work in her stead and still pay her because I sense she needs the money."

"Dr. David look, I don't see how any of this is my business."

"It is. I know you are very protective of her and you are her boss. If you mandate her out of the restaurant for the weekend with full pay, Zarah will yield."

"You don't know Zarah; nobody tells her what to do."

"I know Zarah, you are her boss and guardian and you are firm. Zarah knows that, she will do as you tell her. Even if she fights she will do it." David chuckled.

"You must be a crazy man; you are saying I should kick her out for the weekend for you. Can't you go pick some other girl for your weekend?"

"I want to help her."

"Or you want to help yourself."

"Tom, something is not right with Zarah, she has no business working in your restaurant and I can't help her without having her full attention."

"I see. Her business is better in your bedroom, on your bed?"

"Christ! Are you this twisted? Look Zarah should be the one paying you not the other way round. She is rich, an heir to a major incorporation." There was silence at the other end as Tom reeled with this news. David regretted blurting it out like that. To Tom, his insistence began to make sense now, the puzzle of Zarah just moved into brighter light.

"Hello Tom, are you still there?"

"Yeah. So what happened, why is she here, like this?"

"I just know her Dad died and she came up here afterwards. I want to find out why and I need enough time and your help."

"So I'm just supposed to tell her to get out and go away with you for the weekend."

"Well, putting it that way sounds callous but yes more or less that's what I mean. You know best how to say it."

"Look man, this better be true and yield results. If anything happens to her I will hunt you down and feed you your own flesh piece by piece."

Cold chills ran down David's spine making him swallow hard but he pushed the feeling aside.

"Don't worry; you won't have to do that. Just do your part and you can thank me later."

"You shouldn't be a doctor. You are a rogue like me, if not worse than me and I should hate you. Be here tomorrow by 6:00pm."

"Thanks, I owe you one."

"Get lost." Tom hung up.

David smiled to himself as he replaced the phone. He started humming to himself, tapping his fingers to the rhythm of his hum as he resettled in his seat.

His intercom rang just as he was considering making another phone call.

It was Chloe announcing his 2:00pm appointment. Miss Dew came in all smiles.

"Hi Dr. D."

"Hello Miss Dew, how are you today?"

"Better but still having some pains."

"Hmm…" he nodded.

"I have your test results, they are right here."

Studying the test results for a while, he began to scribe on his prescription sheet as Miss Dew looked on.

"Here, this should take care of your pains. You have a minor urinary tract infection. I'd like to see you again in two weeks to check how you're doing."

"Great, thanks Dr. D."

"You are welcome."

She left and he saw Mr. Clifford was waiting. He walked in, his walking stick in one hand and the other hand pointing at David.

"You better have a good excuse for moving my appointment?"

'Mr. Clifford. Good afternoon and how are you today?'

"I am as good as you left me the last time."

"Come over here and lie down, let me take a look at you."

"Oh, you don't have to. At eighty nine, I am only glad I can get around, come in here and have a fresh conversation with you every other week.'

"But you know I need to document your visit."

"Doctors and their probes," he sighed. "The nurse has checked my blood pressure, my weight and other vital signs, I'm good."

"Yeah, I know but a doctor's got to do what a doctor's got to do," David said smiling.

"Yeah, liking poking and counting my ribs and organs?"

Bursting into laugher."Yes if I must."

After the examination they talked about the weather, David's clinic and when he would be getting married. Mr. Clifford chided him for working too hard and not having enough spare time to mix up and find a decent girl to marry. David just laughed through his scolding.

The rest of the day went as planned but David had one last major chore to carry out before leaving the office. He had written it boldly on paper and tucked it in his pen holder so he would not forget. With his appointments done and his patients' notes finished, he picked up the phone to attend to this last but important chore. Uncle Leo was delighted that David called but wondered what changed.

"Why do I have a feeling this visit is different? You know, you've never called back to remind me that you are still coming out this way."

"Yeah, because you were the one always cornering me into coming over, I knew you would be prepared and awaiting my arrival. But this time I invited myself, so I am making sure you remember."

"David…?"

"Uncle Leo….." David said laughing."

"You are smart but not too smart for old Leo."

"Right, I give up. Actually I am calling to let you know that I will be coming with a guest. I hope it's okay with you?"

"Ha! Your guest is my guest and you are welcome anytime. It's about time young people come away from the hustle and bustle of the city for some time."

"Eh... Yes, I agree, but this guest might require some extra from you and she might not be all that good company because she is not coming willingly. As a matter of fact she doesn't yet know that she is coming your way."

"She..?"

"Yes, she." There was silence at the other end of the phone.

"Uncle, uncle Leo... are you there?"

"Zarah?"

"Yes, Zarah."

"I see, I better get my lazy bones up and about to put the guest room and the rest of the house in order. I will have to go grocery shopping tomorrow. Oh my God, David you should have told me earlier."

"No, no uncle…. Please you don't need to stress yourself. I can clean up the guest room for myself while she gets the room I usually stay in and for the groceries I will shop for some before coming down. Besides we won't be there until a little bit after six in the evening tomorrow."

"Rubbish! I won't have any of that. How many times do I get to have anybody come out here and this time we are talking about a girl." Leo intentionally dragged out the last word. David was sure his uncle was beaming with smiles at his end.

"Uncle Leo, please this is not what you think. She is just an old friend and right now she needs help and a break. I am only trying to be of help."

"Son, you can tell me all about it tomorrow when you come. Right now I have got work to do. So see you tomorrow and have a safe trip as you drive down."

"I don't see why…..'The line went dead. Uncle Leo had hung up. David sat staring and smiling at the phone. It was too late to have second thoughts about this trip but he knew it was not going to be easy with Zarah on one side and Uncle Leo on the other. He only prayed to survive the weekend, he had to go through with his plan.

Chapter 9

Friday had Tom agitated. He hadn't been able to come up with a reason for Zarah to take the weekend off. He had told himself a thousand times that he wasn't selling Zarah, but he couldn't shake off the thought that that was what he was actually doing. He knew he had to come to a decision to do it or reject David's offer so he needed a clear head to think and come up with something.

After a while he notified Zarah that she couldn't take a lunch break since he needed to see her in his office at that time. What he was about to do was a huge sacrifice on his part. It would cost him money but he'd call it health insurance expenditure for his staff and he didn't mind. He only minded about the outcome of this weekend with David for Zarah. David better live up to his words to cause her no harm or else he wouldn't be able to pronounce the name Zarah afterwards.

"Hi Tom, you wanted to see me."

"It's lunch time already? Tom asked, confused for a moment.

"I believe so." Zarah said with a glance at her watch.

"Huh, please sit down."

"Thanks."

"Yes, I needed to talk to you concerning some changes for this weekend. I am sorry it is kind of short notice but I am left with no choice."

"What? Are you firing me?"

"No! Why would you think that?"

"Then please go straight to the point."

"As I was saying," he continued eyeing her, "We will be having some major cleaning and fumigation done here over this weekend in readiness for the health and safety inspectors on Monday, so you will need to vacate your room today at least by 6:00pm." Zarah sat motionless with shock and Tom cursed David under his breath.

"Did you hear anything I said Zarah?"

Nodding "…but where will I go?"

"Ermm…. I have thought of that. Why don't you call up your friend David? He might have a place or an idea that can be of help."

"No!" She stiffened.

"Why not? He seems like a nice guy and besides he knows this area well."

Zarah, swallowing a lump in her throat, began, "So are you saying that I won't earn anything for two days?"

"Three…maybe. No you will be paid in full since it's an impromptu decision and it isn't any of your faults."

"So I resume on Monday?"

"Yes... Monday afternoon. I will need you to clear the store of your things."

"What about the others? Nobody seems to know about this or am I the only one that won't be coming to work this weekend?"

'No, it affects all. I am so sorry for whatever inconveniences this is causing you.'

Shaking her head. "You have no idea what you just did to me."

"You bet I know, oh yes I know. Apart from having a clean and sanitized environment to work in and sleep in, you will soon discover other benefits and come and thank me later. Mind you I am the one losing here. A weekend of no business and yet I will be spending heavily on the services I hired plus the salaries. Please just say you understand, thank me and be on your way back to work. I wouldn't want us wasting more than necessary time on this being that you are leaving by 6:00pm."

Zarah gave him a stare that went right through his soul, stood up and left.

"Damn! Damn you David." Tom swore, banging his fist down hard on most of the files on his table.

Zarah went through the rest of the day in a trance, not able to bring herself to think. Each passing minute felt like a countdown to her death sentence.

David was at The Stone Family Restaurant a little before 6:00pm with Chuzzy. His vet had called to cancel his boarding service because a family emergency had taken him out of town. David had no option than to have him accompany him to Yukon.

Max went pad in hand to David as he sat at a table.

"Good evening sir, how are you today and what can I get for you?"

A little startled, since he hadn't seen Max approach, David looked up at him struck dumb for some seconds as he stared at tattoos that peeped from under his collar and cuffed sleeves. He noted Max's clean shaven head and well-muscled body and wondered briefly how Zarah actually coped with all of these.

Max smiled and tilted his head sideways, raising his eyebrows at David in question while wondering whether David had never seen anyone with tattoos and earrings. David collected himself, licked his lips and muttered "Sorry…can I have iced tea please?"

"Just iced tea?"

"Just iced tea." he nodded.

Half way through his iced tea, Zarah walked past him with a canvass bag slung over her right shoulder. He sprang to his feet, hitting the table and toppling his drink but caught it right before it spilled. He quickly placed a twenty dollar bill on the far left of the table and placed his tea glass over it before running after Zarah.

Tom chuckled from his usual position and muttered "That's not going to be an easy ride, but that's his shot, he asked for It." he turned and went into his office. His phone started ringing almost immediately he sat down and he knew who.

"Yes…?"

"What's up?"

"We cool and you?"

"Cut that shit, you know what I mean."

"Zarah..?"

"Yes, you asshole!"

"Mind your language, will you!"

"Then tell me what I need to know."

"You seem quite interested in Zarah and I don't see how this is your business."

"You made it my business remember? You even pay me for it."

"Oh …thanks for reminding me."

"Spill it, you motherfucker."

"Stop cursing on me if you wanna hear anything."

It was one thing to curse and quite another thing to hear someone else curse on you, it was so irritating. He would so love to hit Lemon right now but he continued into the silence at the other end. Tom told him about David's phone call and his plan.

"So are you really having the cleaning and fumigators come over?"

"Yes actually. This place is indeed due for those."

"And you trust him?"

"I think so…"

"You think so?"

"Come on, stop sounding like a jealous lover."

"I will feed you your balls if you make me come over there!"

"Oh see me, I am shaking. Ha-ha…"

"Idiot!"

Lemon slammed his phone down, furious. Then he wondered whether there was any truth in what Tom had said. Then he questioned his own interest in Zarah. Perhaps it was because of the time he had spent watching her and talking about her. All that seemed about to change now it appeared Tom had a better idea of how to keep her safe and who was he to say otherwise.

*** *** ***

David met Zarah outside leaning on the restaurant's sign post.

"Hi Zarah."

"Hi'. She replied without looking at him. "So, where are you taking me for the weekend?"

"Do you want a surprise or should I tell you?"

Ignoring him, she turned and walked to his car, surprised to see Chuzzy who poked his head out of the window on seeing her. She reached out and stroked his head and Chuzzy responded by licking and inching closer into her hands. David watched as he walked up behind her. Inside the car, he introduced them and told her that Chuzzy rarely meet people so he wasn't very social and his response to her was a first. "You like her, huh?" he turned and teased Chuzzy remembering how he used to groan around Denise. He didn't like Denise and David knew the feeling was mutual. At his teasing tone, Chuzzy got all excited, bringing his head forward to nibble and lick Zarah's ear and the side of her face. She responded by reaching back to stroke and pats his head.

After a few minutes of that, David had to speak sternly, "Cut it out Chuzzy and settle down, you are in a moving car."

Chuzzy whined his displeasure but did as he was told. Zarah showed no reaction as she sat looking straight ahead of her.

"We are going to the outskirt of the town, to my grand-uncle's farm. He is expecting us and be ready to be fussed over because he hardly gets anyone out there. He is Uncle Leo. He loves fishing." Still no response from Zarah.

"You are not going to talk to me, are you?"

Zarah didn't answer; one might as well assume she didn't hear him.

David started humming to himself and when he got tired of hearing his tunes he switched the radio on but all the stations seemed to be playing one love song or the other, so he just slotted in his Michael Smith CD. As soon as the track 'Draw me close to you' started playing he could sense Zarah's discomfort. He wondered why but ignored her. This was far better than the silence or the love songs on the radio.

Soon enough, he pulled up in front of the farm house where Uncle Leo was standing on the front porch waiting and beaming with smiles.

They walked up to him with David greeting him and quickly introducing Zarah. Uncle Leo stretched out his arms to hug her but Zarah recoiled from him muttering a greeting and excuse at the same time. Chuzzy chose that moment to announce his presence, pulling on Uncle Leo's pants. Leo bent down and engulfed Chuzzy in a hug.

"There you are big guy, ensuring I do not go without a hug."

Straightening up, he winked at Zarah who looked away and he patted David who had watched the whole scene.

"Come on in, I have dinner already cooking, it mustn't get burnt."

Turning to Zarah, he added, "Here let me show you to your room. You might want to freshen up before dinner."

He led her to a room at the end of the hallway and opened the door to a softly scented spacious room, saying gently,

"This used to be my wife's room. It's ensuite. I have tried to make it as comfortable as possible but do not hesitate to ask if you need anything. See you at dinner."

Zarah just nodded and took a few steps into the room as the door closed behind her. The room was finished in warm colored paint and soft furnishing. It was lovely; the bed… the bed was so attractive looking, and sported a set of fluffy feathers. She inched closer and touched the bedding, it felt like a mix of silk and cashmere of the softest type she had ever seen. The bathroom was the same, very warm and welcoming. Running her bath she thought the room was very different from the rest of the house, the part she had seen so far. It is nothing like you would think to find in a farm house. She thought that it reminded her of her own room but quickly corrected her thoughts. Her room while being expensively furnished was a contrast to this. This is was mature yet classic, not stuffy, soft and alluring yet brimming with character. She loved it; she loved everything about it. If only it was hers to live in. Settling into the bath she allowed the tears to flow freely. This was the first time she had really cried since after her father's death but even this felt different, it felt freeing. She lingered in the bath loving the refreshing scents and feelings enveloping her, and then she remembered dinner. Taking her time to put on a well-worn cotton blouse and Capri pants, she reluctantly left the room for dinner.

Uncle Leo and David were already seated and waiting at the dining table when she came out. She noted that David had changed into a T-shirt and a pair of Levi's and his hair was still damp but Uncle Leo looked the same. They looked relieved to see her. They must have thought she wasn't going to come out but they should have told her what time dinner was, she thought.

"I'm sorry for keeping you waiting." She muttered to no one in particular.

They both smiled at her and said it was okay. Right then, she felt like she hated them. Why were they so kind and tolerant? Her train of thought was cut short with Uncle Leo's deep crisp voice.

"We are having steak which is David's favorite. Sorry I didn't know what you like to eat so I made some buttery baked potatoes and chicken salad. I hope you will like them."

She felt like screaming at the top of her lungs because that really was her favorite dinner, something she usually ate with her dad. Instead, she just smiled sadly, muttered her thanks and reached for the baked potatoes. Uncle Leo caught her hands midway stopping her from reaching the potatoes.

"Not before we give thanks." Uncle Leo said to her.

Ahh… church folks like Madison, she thought and immediately stilled at the thought of Madison so she snatched her hand away more roughly that she'd intended. She felt like an idiot. What was she doing here with these people, eating and planning to sleep in that scented room, with its soft beautiful bed. She did not belong here. She should just leave. Then she remembered she had no roof over her this weekend. She was a charity case and she was expected to be grateful, no thanks to Madison. She dragged her thoughts back to dinner, she mustn't ruin it with thoughts of that name again. She was hungry and needed to eat. With that she became aware that Uncle Leo was already eating and David was offering her the baked potatoes dish, which she gladly took.

She ate quietly, nodding when asked if she liked the food while listening to David and his Uncle chit-chat about the weather, the farm, his practice and some pastor and the ladies in his church. She was only interested in the meal. The baked potatoes tasted divine, really buttery, the salad very fresh with the chicken savory and meaty. She also had a few bites of steak and that was a delight all its own.

After dinner David saw to the dishes and Uncle Leo left to tidy some things outside. She walked out on the backyard deck not being someone who turned in early. She sat on the stairs overlooking some plants though she couldn't make out if they were flowers or edible plants through the darkness. She knew she liked the scents out here.

Sitting and staring out in the dark reminded her of her usual spot for night breaks in the restaurant, without the stray cats and no thoughts of time but the thoughts of her plans refused to be conjured. It must be the food or the smells; they were messing with her mind. Uncle Leo came out with two glasses of golden colored drinks and handed her one.

"No thanks, I don't drink alcohol."

"Me neither, this is fresh apple juice"

"Oh ok, thanks!"

She took the glass he held to her and sipped, feeling like hugging him, it tasted so good. They both sat staring out into the darkness.

"I like my room, thanks for having me."

"Glad you like it. It hasn't been opened in the past ten and half years."

"After your wife died?"

"Yes, after Maria died. She died of breast cancer. It was a long struggle and in her last days she desired some level of quietness and isolation. So we had to do up that room where she could be without hearing the goings-on in the house.'

"Sorry to hear that."

"Oh it's all right. Maria died long before her actual death."

"What do you mean?"

"You see we had only a son, he grew to become a lawyer. He died a week before his wedding from a drug overdose. We never suspected and the shock killed Maria long before the cancer."

"What about the would-be bride? She must have been heartbroken too."

"Nancy? We never knew. I remember she got married not too long afterwards and divorced within two years. She was a model, never wanted kids as we heard then."

"It must have been hard on you, burying your loved ones. Did Nancy come for her fiancé's funeral?"

"No."

"Hmm….she couldn't bear it, I guess."

"Don't think so."

"Why?"

"I always suspected it was more out of fear of our reaction. It's speculated that she introduced him to drugs, but I say my son was old enough and free to make a choice."

"And he chose drugs, huh?"

"And he chose drugs."

"You don't hold it against her?"

"No."

She looked away, lost in thought.

"I heard your parents are dead?"

She nodded.

"You must be missing them?"

"I do."

"Well thank God you still have your step mom as I heard, I guess God made sure you were not left alone in this world."

Zarah remained silent, swallowing the hard lump that seemed to have suddenly formed in her throat. Uncle Leo was looking at her and noting her reaction, smiled to himself and continued as if he didn't notice he'd touched a sore point.

"You know David is like a son to me, his father was born about the same time as my son. Of all my nieces and nephews, I seem to have formed a bond with David. Don't get me wrong, I love all the others, they come by once in a long while but I always look forward to having David around. It's a great pleasure to me having you around. It's been a long while any female graced this house over-night. So my dear you are most welcome. Feel free around here.'

"Thank you, though I still feel like I'm taking advantage of you. It was fear that made me come down with David. I had planned sleeping on the street after the 'eviction notice' from Tom, but one look at the street when I came out of the restaurant, I got clueless and scared. I am really grateful."

"Don't worry, it's nothing. Now it's really getting late and it can be mighty cold out here. David had already retired to his room."

"Oh, okay. I must be on my way to bed then. I must have lost track of time."

"We did dear."

"Thanks again for dinner, it was wonderful."

"You're welcome!"

They went in and Zarah went straight to her room, having a strong urge all of a sudden to lay on the soft bed. The bed yielded its promises of comfort and luxury and enveloped her as if it had been waiting to hug her. She slept off instantly as her head hit the pillows.

Chapter 10

There was a brief moment of silence as Madison walked into the lobby of Harrison Towers. It made her remember the last gossip she heard about herself from Paul. That she had gone insane and locked herself up in her house for fear of people, even daylight. Just before the door of the elevator closed, she smiled broadly at all the curious eyes and waved. That was bound to blow up the gossip, she laughed. She walked into the Harrison board room at exactly 10:00 am where all the executives and Christy were already seated and waiting for her. Except for Christy, the reaction she got from the others was the same as that she'd got from people in the lobby. Christy started the briefing after all the hellos, how-are-you-doings and smiles had been shared. It was very brief and straight to the point, Christy's style. Madison expressed how happy and eager she was to start work and gently warned that they could expect a few changes and reshuffling. She asked that within the next two weeks every head of department should put together a report for the last four years and schedule a time to take her through it. She sensed they were still in shock or awe because nobody reacted to what she said. She was shown to her office, 'the CEO's office', after the meeting. The office was as Sam had left it. She circled the table to the huge chair behind it, running her two right middle fingers on the large chestnut table. She sat in the chair, taking in the entire office section by section and noting the spot where she had been shown Sam fell. She decided the office was too masculine; she would have to remodel it. She got up and went to the adjourning office - the secretary's office and decided to start her remodeling from there. The room would be redone to accommodate two persons; a secretary and a personal assistant. The CEO's waiting lounge too wouldn't be left out. Everything would have to go but not the files. Those, she would immediately start to go through. She acknowledged the beautiful and expensive layout of the office but knew she didn't want its masculine overpowering nature. She would keep the chestnut table, its chair and the book shelves but every other thing would go, from the paintings to the coffee set. She would completely redesign the office to something modern, soft and classy. Very importantly she needed more light in there; natural or artificial. She picked up the phone and called two different interior decorators to come in and make their assessments that day.

Some minutes later the office phone rang and it was Mr. Williams, one of the directors requesting a meeting with Madison. She scheduled him for 2:00pm and quickly called the reception downstairs to instruct them to send her visitors straight up to her. In thirty minutes, an agent from Lush Homes and Offices was announced. Harry was his name. He noted all the details Madison wanted, asking questions here and there for clarification. He completed his assessment, taking pictures section by section. She told him she wanted the cost and 3D presentation by noon the following day and if approved, she would like the work to start the day after, Wednesday and be completed by Friday. He took all that down. An hour later the consultant from Colour Code came in. Anna, a cheery sweet lady in her mid-thirties. Madison loved her instantly and prayed that she would be the one who could best interpret her ideas for the offices. Anna, like the agentfrom Lush Homes and Offices, took down notes and measurements and took sectional pictures of the offices. She got the same instructions for the work as the Lush agent had been given.

Madison was ready and waiting by 2:00pm for Mr. Williams who walked in out of breath probably from the short walk from the elevator to her office. Mr. Williams looked totally overweight and she thought he probably did no form of exercise. She watched him more or less pushing his tummy in front of him in a bid to walk until he was seated in front of her. Madison made a mental note to discuss his weight issues with him after she had settled in. The company met its responsibility to provide his health insurance, so he had to keep up his own end by keeping healthy.

"Good afternoon Mr. Williams."

"Good afternoon Mrs. Harrison. How are you today?"

"I am good and you?"

"I am good too" Madison doubted it. "Thanks for asking."

"What can I do for you please?"

"Nothing really, I just came to welcome you formally to the company and ask if there is anything I can do to help you settle in much quicker."

"Okay, thanks but I can't think of anything right now that I can't handle." She said, flashing him her sweetest smile.

"Oh wait a minute, I know, please tell HR department to put out an urgent advert or go through their archives and interview for a secretary and personal assistant, preferably ladies. This should be done before Friday, because I will be doing the final interview on Friday, so they should short list at least three candidates for each position to me."

"But Madam, Mr. Harrison's secretary is still here, she can be moved back to her formal office for you."

"No thanks, I prefer some new persons."

"And two?"

"Yes two. Do you have any problem with that?"

"No, not at all, just wondering, you know you mentioned something about reshuffling and I thought bringing Rosa back as the CEO's secretary could be a part of it."

"Well, you leave the reshuffling to me Mr. Williams. But I promise you will be the first to know before any is done."

"Okay and no layoffs?" he asked, twisting his fingers in his lap.

"Will there be any need for that?"

"No, I am just asking?"

"Good, if you have no other concerns, I wouldn't want to keep you from your duties in your office."

Madison had her hand extended for a hand shake and her brightest smile in place. Mr. Williams nodding and rising took her extended hand in a hand shake whilst trying hard to hide his displeasure. Madison watched him leave with the same effort he used to come in. She would remember to include him on her to-watch list and check his personnel file.

In the elevator, Mr. Williams decided he did not like Mrs. Harrison. It was hard enough accepting her as his CEO but dismissing him like that from her office was belittling. She forgot he was the reason she still had something to come back to after her four years of self-pity, insanity, plotting and what have you. She might be Mrs. Harrison and this might be Harrison Inc. but he did not have to like her.

Tuesday at 11.55am, a Mr. Frank from Lush Homes and Offices turned up at reception and asked to see Madison. On appearing before her, he explained that he was actually from their marketing department and was in charge of presentations while Harry was on the technical team. Madison offered him a seat and wondered why both of them didn't just come for the assessment. She doubted this Frank could present a remodeling for offices he did not assess. She felt disappointed with Lush Homes and Offices. Anna was announced at exactly 12:00noon so Madison decided they would both make their presentations to her. During the presentations, she thought Lush Homes and Offices was good but felt no connection with their redesigning idea. Colour Code got it though; it felt like Anna was taking her on a walk through the corridors of her mind. She tried hard to restrain herself from showing any emotion throughout both presentations. She gave the signed checks for the balance of their assessment and designing fee and told them she needed some time to think but would contact them before 3:00pm with a decision.

Few minutes after they left, Madison called the manager of Color Code.

"Hello Miss Irene, this is Mrs. Harrison of Harrison Inc."

"Hi Mrs. Harrison. I hope everything is okay?"

"Very well actually, I am calling to inform you that I loved every bit of what Anna presented to me a few minutes ago. You have got to start work tomorrow at Harrison Towers."

"That's wonderful! Thanks for choosing us."

Madison could literally feel the manager's victory dance, and smiled at her end, "Yes. As for payment, I would like to pay the deposit but please remember the discount."

"Very well, like I promised, you will be having a 25% discount off your $7500 bill. Please hang on while I connect you with the finance department to process your 50% deposit. Will there be anything else?"

"Yes please, will Anna be part of the team doing the redesigning?"

"Yes she will. She is to make sure everything goes as assessed and estimated."

"Good, I like that. Now I can pay."

She finished the payment, hung up and dialed Lush Homes and Offices. The marketing manager picked up.

"Hello George, this is Mrs. Harrison of Harrison Inc."

"Hello Mrs. Harrison. Did you find everything ok?"

"Yes I did, I liked the design Frank presented very much however, I am sorry I didn't find a connection to it and moreover I didn't like the idea that Harry who did the assessment didn't do the presentation. These are my thoughts though. I had given Frank a check for the balance of the assessment and designing fee."

"Oh really. If that is the case we can still send Harry to come do the presentation."

"Not to bother, I have contracted another firm. Just thought to let you know. Thanks."

"Fine then, goodbye!"

"Goodbye!"

"That's done." Madison said reclining in her seat, happy. She was happy that Color Code got the contract. She knew she was being prejudiced but did not care. She liked the fact that Color Code was owned by a woman and Anna reminded her of herself before her marriage to Sam. Women are supposed to stick up for each other and stick together, she concluded with a smile.

By Friday Madison's office was done and dusted. Her new staff were hired to resume on Monday. The speed of her actions set tongues wagging and emotions flaring, but she ignored all that and focused on gearing up for her planned reshuffling. She had read the files of all the employees in Harrison Inc. and decided not to fire anyone but had penned down some names for investigation. It looked like Paul would have his job back. Mr. William was extremely annoyed over the redesigning of the CEO's office but couldn't express it since Madison made no demands on Harrison Inc. finances. He did not think she needed to erase all traces of Sam from the office, like he didn't matter. Christy was also felt emotional conflict. She talked with Mr. William, whose fawning she enjoyed. They both felt strongly attached to the memory of Sam and felt Madison's actions were a betrayal. They questioned why she came back now after all these years and what really happened to Zarah, even Sam. They decided Madison would not get away with her scheming.

By the next Monday, Madison had set bi-monthly targets for each department. She shocked everyone with the introduction of a new business line; health supplements. There were arguments from the heads of departments and the directors that Harrison Inc. was a cosmetic corporation not a pharmaceutical company. She agreed but asked what was the use of developing products for outside of the body without caring what went inside. She projected that the supplements could even help the cosmetics since they aimed at repairing, enhancing and maintaining the body. She left the business development department with two-week duration to come up with the first product.

The week went better than she anticipated. Madison surprised herself with her adjustment to the position of CEO at Harrison Inc. Having what to do took her mind of Zarah and Sam. Her new staff were superb, knowing their duties and functions well. She believed strongly that hiring them was the best thing. She could hardly believe that she was in a new week already. Everything was going so well and she was looking forward to the management meeting which she had rescheduled for noon, because of the Bridge Company. Mathew and his son, Joel of the

Bridge Company came by to pay a courtesy call and welcome her to her new duties. Madison, on taking up the running of Harrison Inc. had written to all their partners and business associates of her new position as CEO. Just as she was settling in to resume what she had been doing before the Bridge Company's visit, her Personal Assistant (PA) informed her that a Mr. Paul was waiting to see her though she couldn't find him in her appointment book.

"Oh yes, I forgot to mention it, please let him in." Madison said and Paul was shown in.

"I suppose you have a good reason for being here without appointment?"

"I should think so too, Mrs. Harrison." Paul said as he sat down in front of her slipping a note towards her.

Madison read the note and looked up at him in a panic but Paul as cool as ever just smiled and nodded while telling her how beautiful her office is. Madison did as the note said and turned up her TV volume. Her secretary rushed in.

"Mrs. Harrison is everything okay?"

"Mm' smiling sweetly, "please no more interruptions. Thank you."

"I'm sorry." Jane left and locked the door from her side.

"Yes, what is it?" Madison asked in a muffled voice.

"Relax, it is nothing serious. I just wanted to alert you to something."

"What?"

"Do you know you are being investigated again?"

"By whom?"

He gave her a knowing look.

"Homicide unit? But for what?"

"The thing is, Christy and Mr. William happened to mention your sudden action of taking over everything. They are insinuating you killed Sam, made away with Zarah, waited for the whole thing to die down while you played the bereaved. Now, thinking it is the right time you have come to claim your prize."

"What? And you believe this nonsense?"

He stared at her for a moment, taking his time with taking off his hat and placing it on the edge of the table. Then, getting her full attention he said, "No!"

"Then?"

Paul stood up and walked to the bookshelves, admiring the shelf accessories and books.

"I think your house and this office are wired. Phones too might have been compromised."

"That's ridiculous, I haven't done anything wrong, and how can they possibly think up such nonsense?"

"They can and they have."

"They can't find anything on me. I am not the black widow."

"You never can tell."

"What did you just say?"

"Cool off; you have to see anything can mean anything to someone looking for something. Just be careful."

Madison just swallowed hard to control her anger as Paul continued.

"I understand Mr. William is one of the directors here. It is possible he is just genuinely concerned and others too."

"Others? Like hell they are!"

"I have asked you to cool off. Blowing off isn't gonna help you in this. Besides this is only an investigation, no one is accusing you of anything."

"And you? What's your take on this?"

Paul turned slowly to face her fully.

"I know you are innocent, I checked you out when I was working for you."

"So I was paying you to check me out? No wonder you had no result on Zarah."

There was a cold moment of silence. Paul coughed breaking the silence.

"It will do you well to act like you do not know about this. Treat your director well, you know, a little friendlier. I heard you are not. I will see you next week Monday at this time and please do schedule me in your appointment book this time.'

"How much is this going to cost me?"

Putting on his hat Paul said, "I believe I owe you some favors and besides I am not making any effort at this. Some of those homicide guys are my drinking buddies and they are expecting my help on the case. Good day Mrs. Harrison …and the television is too loud, don't you think?"

With a tilt of his hat he walked out of Madison's office.

Chapter 11

Zarah woke up to meet Chuzzy at her door as she opened it. He nudged her legs in greeting when she stepped out, so she bent and stroked his back in response. Chuzzy led the way waddling in front towards the kitchen where David and Uncle Leo were chatting.

"Good morning."

"Good morning." Both echoed.

"I hope you slept well?" David asked.

"Yes I did, better than I have done in years."

The two men exchanged knowing glances.

"Come sit here close to me." Uncle Leo said pointing at the breakfast table as girl and dog walked towards it.

"What will you have for breakfast?"

"Anything you guys have left."

"Nothing. We have eaten and didn't know what you might like and Uncle Leo insisted he wants you to have your choice."

"That's right." Uncle Leo said.

"Anything will do really." Zarah answered.

"So, bacon and toast will be okay?"

"Yes please."

"Coffee or juice?"

"Juice…..the type you gave me yesterday night." She said to Uncle Leo.

"Ah…yes, you will get that with all pleasure." Uncle Leo stood up to attend to his promise.

"You know I can fix the toast and bacon myself?" Zarah asked David who just nodded and ignored her. One part of her hated them and the other part was thrilled to indulge in the pampering.

'What will you like to do today?' Uncle Leo asked Zarah.

"I wish I had come with the novel I bought five months ago, this would have been a perfect time to read it."

"You forgot it?" David continued.

"No, I had thought I would be sleeping on the streets."

"Why?" David asked eyes popping.

"I was annoyed that Tom chose to clean at your convenience, so I was determined not to give you the satisfaction of coming with you. But one look at the streets, I gave in."

The men roared with laughter and Zarah couldn't help not joining them.

"So?" David continued.

She just shrugged.

"Well," Uncle Leo chipped in. "I was thinking you might like to see the farm, I can take you round."

"That would be nice." Her face lit up.

"I must warn you, it's pretty large."

"I can imagine." She replied.

"Great so we will leave the fishing to David. His grilled fish is the bomb. You must taste it but he will have to catch the fish first."

"You bet!" David replied.

"We must hurry up then before the sun gets too hot." Uncle Leo said placing her glass of Apple juice before her.

"Zarah, you know you don't have to go with Uncle Leo." David said.

"I don't have to go with anyone. I just want to be left alone," she thought, suddenly feeling the need to regain control of her life. Things were moving too fast, she was almost losing herself but she only smiled and said she was looking forward to walking the farm.

"Well youth doesn't always hold the charm David." Uncle said winking at Zarah.

"Yeah right, you should know better I am sure." David restored.

Zarah ignored them and ate her toast and bacon in silence.

After breakfast, Zarah did the dishes then David excused himself to go get ready for his fishing. He came out calling on Chuzzy for company. Uncle Leo followed him watching closely.

"David, are you not forgetting something?"

"Nope. I am all set."

"Your fishing rod and ice cooler?"

"Don't need those today." He said, humming a tune to himself."

"Then you are not going fishing, are you?" He asked David with a wide grin on his face.

Grinning back at Uncle Leo, David said; "You will surely have grilled fish for dinner."

"Rogue!"

David gave him a mock salute and drove off. Inside Uncle Leo found that Zarah had left for her room. He went in to get dressed for the walk.

Leo took Zarah to his chicken run, the piggery, the cowshed, the vegetable farm, his orchard and finally the stables. One horse in particular was Uncle Leo's show off; his 'Orlov trotter mare'. A pure breed, with a glossy black coat, a white circle around one eye, and traces of white on its tail gave her a unique and beautiful appearance.

"Here, meet Amanda my favorite of all the horses. She is a thoroughbred of Russian origin."

Sure indeed she is Russian, I can even smell it. Zarah thought.

"Yeah, I can see. Quite arrogant, too self-assured I would say."

"Arrogant? No. I would say confident, more like telling you I have your back."

Zarah turned her face away as if to hide her thoughts from Uncle Leo, since she was thinking that all things Russian like Madison are the same, arrogant, wicked and self-absorbed. But Uncle Leo seemed to have a different idea. Funny life coincidences.

"Do you ride?"

"Huh?"

"I asked if you ride."

"No."

"Good! Amanda is just right for you. She is the perfect horse for you. She is the perfect horse any old man could wish for at any time."

"But I don't have to ride."

"That's if you are going back to the house alone because I am going out to the field to check the fence on the far side."

"Can't I just stick around?"

"Do you really want to do that or you are just afraid of riding?"

"No, it's just that I hate anything Russian and do not want to ride Amanda," Zarah felt like shouting at the top of her voice but she kept quiet.

"Now, come on child. I haven't got all day. I will steady her while you mount."

"Which horse are you riding?"

"Aldo here, a mixed breed. Gentle old soul like me. He is the oldest of all my horses."

"I hope I don't fall off, I told you I don't know how to ride."

"You don't have to do anything. I will lead and hold her reins. She will follow."

"Hmmm, like Madison to follow a lead?" She imagined, with her face twisted sarcastically.

"Bad thoughts?" Uncle Leo asked looking at her.

"Nothing," she blushed.

They went down to the part of the fence where Uncle Leo had received reports that it was threatening to fall. On the way he pointed out his worker's quarters, his store, and the trucks that made deliveries to town. Madison was amazed at how huge the farm really was. Seeing Uncle Leo this way was different and it gave her a new respect and admiration for him.

"You know Amanda really likes you, she doesn't allow just about anyone to mount her."

Zarah looked down at Amanda and felt like patting her but held herself back.

David was already back from fishing and in the kitchen cleaning the fish when they got back to the house.

"Hi, I just made fresh cold lemonade to quench your thirst and lunch is ready when you guys are." David told them as they came in.

"Thanks Dave, you are a blessing. I could do a barrel of that." They laughed

"You are welcome Zarah! Uncle Leo how about you?"

"I would have preferred some apple juice but I will make do with lemonade, thanks!"

Eating lunch, they chatted about how David chickened out of fishing but Zarah could guess they both knew he wasn't going to go fishing in the first place.

After dinner Uncle Leo took his favorite position on his rocking chair, rocking to and fro while reading the papers he missed in the morning. Zarah opted to do the dishes while David sat by the kitchen counter.

"I heard you rode a horse for the first time today, how was it?"

"Surprisingly great despite my earlier assessment of Amanda."

"Huh. I bet you were expecting her to throw you off after such comments?"

"You heard too?"

"Yep." He nodded.

"Well yes, I half expected her to do so."

"But she didn't?"

"Mm-mm... She didn't."

"You see, you judged her too quickly without giving her a chance."

Zarah grew still for a moment and murmured "Whatever that means."

"Sorry, I was only thinking out loud." David said.

There was silence as Zarah dried the plates and put them back in the cabinets.

"You guys must excuse me; I will be going to bed now. I thought I would have been able to grab a wink this afternoon but that didn't happen and I am still raw from the horse ride.'

"Are saying you regret the outing?" Uncle Leo asked putting down his papers.

"No, not at all." Zarah jumped to defend herself. "In fact, I must thank you for the experience and you have a really beautiful farm but I honestly was hoping to have as much rest as I could this weekend."

"It's alright my child, I was just teasing you. Good night and have a restful sleep."

"Good night, but remember we will be going to the 8:30am service tomorrow morning.' David said.

"What?" Zarah half screamed.

'Service…. Church, you know tomorrow is Sunday." David said.

"Oh … I didn't realize… I mean… Good night." She blurted out and stormed off with Chuzzy at her heels.

"Chuzzy, say your good night at the door." David called after Chuzzy.

Chuzzy indeed said his goodnight at the door, he stopped and sat at the door with his head tilted up as Zarah patted and stroked him good night.

Climbing into the soft bed with the hope of sleeping off immediately like the night before never happened. Zarah instead found herself musing over the day's events. She thought of Amanda, 'Russians being kind', the farm, Uncle Leo... a cunning pushy but kind old soul, Chuzzy. David... she seemed to lack words for David but she acknowledged that he was becoming more than she would like to admit, and then the church. Church! How could she have missed that? She go to church? When last had she been in any church? Six years ago to be exact. Wouldn't God do to her what she had hoped he should have done to Madison? Maybe at last the Bible would prove itself. She could already see headlines in the papers; "The Bible is fulfilled in our times: the grounds opened and swallowed Zarah Harrison for daring to come into a church after six years of absence and planning murder."

No, she was not going. She should have known that as church folks, Uncle Leo and David would be going to church during this weekend. She would have to wake up sick tomorrow. She kept phrasing and rephrasing her excuses until she fell asleep.

*** *** ***

"Have you been able to figure out what her problem is?" Uncle Leo asked David when he heard Zarah close her room door.

"No, and you?"

"Me neither. But I sense it is hatred and grudge at her step mom. Did you say she is Russian?'

"Half Russian."

"Hmm… I see."

"What?"

"Nothing."

Sighing, David got to his feet. "Good night Uncle Leo, I must be off to bed. Come on Chuzzy say your good night."

Chuzzy took a step towards Uncle Leo before turning to follow David, waddling and waggling his tail.

Sunday morning, Zarah woke up as if there was an alarm at her head. Try as she might, she couldn't come up with any excuse for not getting ready for church. She failed woefully at her attempts. She reluctantly got ready mindful of time but all the while feeling like a ram being led to the slaughter.

At the service the pastor's message came too close for her comfort. He started off with a topic Zarah did not pay attention to but eventually veered into analyzing the weight of a grudge. Zarah didn't like it and though she tried to not listen, she found herself being hit by every single word of the pastor. She was uncomfortable till they got home and she immediately excused herself to her room saying that she might sleep through lunch so they shouldn't wait for her.

Uncle Leo and David spent the afternoon lazing about, talking about this and that until dinner.

Zarah came out early enough for dinner and even joined David in cooking it. They had smoked pork with chicken pea salad. After dinner, she took her leave to the backyard deck as she thought to have one last look and smell of the flowers. David and Chuzzy joined her when he was done with the dishes. Chuzzy sat by her and she stroked his head.

"The sky is clear tonight, I can see the stars," David said.

"Yes I can even make out the flowers or maybe, it's because I now know what they are and where they are."

"No you are right, one can. What do you do in your spare time?"

"I don't have any."

"Quite true. But wouldn't you like to have some? She shrugged her shoulders.

"Why the restaurant, why are you working there?"

"I have told you, that was all I could find and they are good to me.'

"I know, but why? What happened to your degree?"

"I don't have it."

"But you finished?"

"Yes"

"And...? Come on Zarah."

"I owe some fees, so they withheld my certificate."

"How come you owed?"

"I told you my father died."

"But your step mom..."

"Stop calling her that." She said with clenched teeth interrupting David.

"Fine but what went wrong?"

"He died and she took everything."

"It can't be. Your dad wouldn't have left you without an inheritance."

"Yes he did, Harrison Inc. but I wasn't supposed to access it or take over until I had finished my professional exams. So you see the only way to make sure I don't take those exams is to make sure I don't finish school."

"But the will must have had an upkeep plan for you."

"None that I know of."

"But when it was read, why didn't you ask questions?"

"We were read the Will differently and I was only told that I would be fine just like always until I am ready to take over. I know my Dad placed me on some sort of allowance but all of a sudden the money stopped coming. I approached the lawyers and they said I should go to her, which I did and she literally shunned me."

"So you left home after school?"

She nodded.

"Why Yukon?"

"Maybe I just wanted to be lost at the time."

"You plan to go back?"

Her heart skipped a beat before answering.

"Yes, when I make enough to offset the fees but as it is, it will take forever."

David felt her sorrow and for the first time he had to acknowledge that he had some feelings beyond curiosity towards her. He didn't know exactly what but was sure he did not feel pity. His feelings were warm and endearing. Zarah had always been a warm, engaging and smart girl. He had always liked her because she had no airs about her unlike the other rich kids she used to hang around with. But to think she was faced with a situation like this and couldn't handle it broke his heart. He almost put his arms around her to comfort her for all the years of sorrow but he held himself back. He couldn't understand why she gave in so easily. Was she depressed, still grieving or could it simply be the hate she felt for her step mom? She couldn't even say her name. He remembered one of his many visits with his friends to Zarah's house. Her step mom had come out to sayhello and had asked if they needed anything but Zarah had snapped back that she knew where to get anything they might need before any of them could answer. They had all exchanged glances at her outburst but she had continued as if nothing happened. It had felt strange back then and now he recalled the incident, it still begged an answer.

He knew he had to help her. There had to be a way for her to make enough money to go back, pay those fees and get her certificate. And he would have to find out what happened, how the step-mom was able to get away with this kind of fraud.

"If you find a different and better job, will you take it up?"

"Like I had not tried, huh?"

"You must have, I know, but will you take it?"

"Sure." She smiled sadly.

They left Uncle Leo's Monday morning. Zarah and Chuzzy were reluctant but David kept checking the time before their departure. At The Stones Family Restaurant, Zarah could tell there had been a major clean up. She was impressed at how clean everywhere was. Tom was pleased to see Zarah and noticed how refreshed she looked. There even seem to be a glitter in those dark eyes of hers, he thought. He told Zarah to see him when she had settled in.

Chapter 12

David was grateful he had asked Chloe to make Monday as light as possible starting 11.am to 3:30pm and he was happy to hear his 1:00pm appointment cancelled. So at 1:00pm he called Heritage Chartered Accountants and asked to be put through to the HR manager, Mr. John Green.

"Hello Dr. David!" John said as he came on the phone.

"Hello John, how are you doing today?"

"Great, you?"

"Doing well."

"What can I do for you today?"

"I would like to make a withdrawal on the many favors you owe me."

"Okay, what will that be?"

"I have an accountant who needs a job."

There was silence on the other end for a while.

"Actually we are not hiring for now."

"I never asked you if you were hiring, I said I want to make a withdrawal from my favor bank with you."

"Dr. David, I really wish I could help you on this. You see, we do not have any openings now."

"This girl is an asset and you won't be paying as much as you are thinking. She is a recent graduate."

"She can come on our internship program."

"No!"

"Dr. David, I …."

"You will take her as a full staff but I must warn you she doesn't have any certificate to show for her education."

"What you are asking for is huge and very weird. How on earth am I supposed to employ someone with no certificate? What is the proof that she is an accountant?"

"I am the proof. We were in school together and she was a straight 'A' student but unfortunately she couldn't pay her last fees so they withheld her certificate. She needs the job so she can pay up and get the certificate."

"This is huge. I don't really see how I can enlist her as our staff without a certificate."

"I will make a deal with you. Give her a chance to work with you for six months; do not enlist her as a staff. I will enlist her as mine and pay her but she will work with you. After six months, if she is good you will enlist her and pay her as an experienced accountant."

"Why would you pay someone who is not working for you?"

"I like that you are smart. She will be working for me in your office. My retainer-ship with you will be suspended for the six months that I will be paying her."

"You really have thought this through, huh? But you forgot that the office space, equipment and utilities are ours."

"What's your fee?"

"Let me sleep on this, talk to the General Manager and call you back later."

"Tomorrow before 1:00pm please."

"Okay then."

Having no doubt of the outcome of his conversation with John Green, he went ahead and put a call to Tom.

"Hi Tom it's me David."

"Yes of course, I have been waiting for this call."

"That's right. I needed to sort out some stuff as I came in. Thanks for the weekend. I will send out the check today."

"I hope you found out what you wanted."

"Yes I did and that leads me to this. Zarah might be leaving you come Saturday. I haven't spoken to her yet but she indicated interest in moving to something in the area of what she studied at school."

"I helped you for a weekend and this is how you want to pay me back?"

"Not at all. Remember the main reason for the weekend was to find a way to help her."

"Yeah." Tom exhaled loudly. "Who am I to say no? It's her life and I wish her well but we will surely miss her. Should I ask her or…."

"No, no please. I will be there on Wednesday."

"Okay, see you then."

David, happy with himself dialed the intercom for Chloe to tell her about making 1:30 pm available for him on Wednesday, and that he planned to take his break from that time and close early. Next, he called up a realtor requesting their help to find a studio apartment on North May Avenue and other environs near Heritage Chartered Accountants.

On Wednesday, armed with the affirmation of a job for Zarah, David drove to Yukon. He was seated by

6:00pm at a table near one of the windows. He noticed that on seeing him Zarah walked up to him as a friend not as a costumer she needed to serve.

"Hi Dave, what a surprise! I didn't know you were coming. Is everything okay?"

"Yes, I'm sorry, I didn't tell you I was coming but I would like to see you."

"Oh I'm working; I don't know that I can get off"

"Why don't you ask Tom?"

"Tom?" Giving him a suspicious look, she walked off in the direction of Tom's office. Few seconds later she was back at David's table with a look on her face David couldn't interpret.

"I have got 30mins, so shoot."

"Won't you sit down?"

She sat opposite him.

"How are you doing?"

"Get to the point David."

"Right, then. I was able to get you something in an accounting firm and you are to start on Monday."

It took Zarah a moment; she reclined in her seat and studied David's face before replying.

"Already? That was quick. Working as what?"

"Working as an actual accountant but a new recruit."

"Hm. Can I think about it?"

"I thought we discussed this the last time. I had planned to come and pick you on Saturday."

"What about Tom, How will he take it?"

"He knows and he is fine with it."

"You have told him?"

"Yeah, I called him on Monday."

They sat in silence studying each other, until Zarah broke the silence.

"Tell me. What else have you been discussing with him that I do not know of?"

"Nothing."

"I see, I still insist on thinking it over and telling Tom myself, and as we are still on it, what happens to my accommodation, will I have to live in the office?"

"Not at all. I should have a studio apartment ready before Saturday."

"Really. And how am I supposed to pay for that?"

"Zarah, you will be having a $25 an hour job and will be working 8-10 hours a day. You will be able to pay for your apartment. I will pay the initial deposit of three months' rent which you will repay every month. Is that okay?"

"Kind of. It sounds okay but I will still have to think about it."

"Fine, but I will be here by 10:00am Saturday unless I get your call not to come."

"Fine."

"Okay then. I should be on my way."

"Yep, I'm due back at work. Thanks anyway." She got up and left for Tom's office.

Confronting Tom was useless. He just looked at her like she was out of her mind and when she was done with her rant, he told her to let him know what her decision was by the next day then calmly went back to what he was doing before her interruption.

At around twelve on Saturday Zarah found herself in her new apartment on Northwest 140th street. She couldn't believe that was there as a bonafide renter of a studio apartment.

"How much do I owe at the end of the month?"

"$450!"

That would be easy with a $25 an hour job. Thankfully, she had learned to go without a lot of things. So she would still be on track to return to Santa Monica to settle everything once and for all.

Zarah started her job at Heritage Chartered Accountants on Monday. It was a dream come true. She opted for weekly pay. Working 8 hours a day gave her $1000 at the end of each week. It had been a very long time she saw anything near this amount at a time. With good planning, she could go back in less than three months. Plan established and target set, she made up her mind to visit the Emoss on the following Saturday. She had to make the acquaintance of the group especially of their leader and the sooner the better.

Lemon was taken aback when he saw Zarah standing at the entrance of the Emoss club house, sticking out like a sore thumb. Spot was already edging his way toward her with a stagger suggesting he was already high on whatever he'd been taking. Lemon quickly called on Spot to back off as he walked up to Zarah himself.

"What are you doing here?" Lemon asked through clenched teeth to intimidate Zarah, but if it worked she didn't show it.

"I want to see you."

"Me?"

"Yeah."

"Does Tom know that you are here?"

"No, and I don't want him to."

"I see. Come."

He led her to the far right corner, to a private bar. The guys and ladies there got up and left as they approached. Lemon wondered what brought her to him. Well he would soon find out.

"So what can I do for you?" he asked as they were seated.

"I just felt I should get to know you better now that I have a bit more time. I'm Zarah by the way." She extended her right hand.

"Lemon." He said shortly, shaking hands..

Was she daft? What did she mean by, 'to get to know him'? Did she know where she was, what getting to know him meant?

"Are you sure you really want to know me? I am all about drugs, fights, guns and sex." Lemon said leering at her, subconsciously thinking to scare her off.

Zarah caught her breath but guns, oh guns. They really have guns? She thought.

"I believe everything takes getting used to."

"Really?"

"Really!"

"Sooo… I could offer you something to sniff then."

He snapped his fingers in the air all the while watching a frozen Zarah. Jamie brought a small serving plate with tiny wrapped packages on it and a small steel spatula. He cleared the table before him, unwrapped a package and poured its white powdery contents on the table in front of him. He took the spatula, stirred it through the powder then cut lines through it. He bent and took it all in one sniff. Zarah broke out in sweat. Lemon raised his head, wiped the white substance off the tip of his nose and upper lip while offering Zarah another wrap. He broke out in laughter when Zarah stared at his extended hand in horrified shock.

"Right, that's a little too much huh? Come let's try something else."

He rose up and Zarah followed. Walking lazily, he led her through a narrow dark corridor with rooms on either side of it. Muffled animal like sounds could be heard coming from the rooms. Lemon opened one of the doors and stepped in holding the door open for her. He closed the door behind her as she entered and pushed her on the unmade bed that stank of sweat and whatever else had been left behind by its last user. She lay back slowly, anticipating the worst. Drugs were one thing but sex she knew, how bad it could be. Lemon slowly unbuckled his belt and unzipped his jeans. Pulling off his T-shirt, he threw himself down on Zarah but steadied himself with his hands out stretched on either side of her while he lay full length over her. Zarah inhaled a stuttering breath and squeezed her eyes shut. With his face hovering over hers he told her to open her eyes. He stared down at her breathing heavily, intentionally. He feigned going down completely on her but pulled back as Zarah turned her face away with eyes squeezed shut. He sighed and rolled over. He got off the bed, zipped up his jeans and buckled his belt. Grasping her with one hand and picking his T-shirt with the other, he threw it over his left shoulder. He shoved her carelessly into the corridor still grasping her arm tightly until they got to the main entrance. He shoved her out the door.

"Go home Princess, go home to where you belong. Anywhere but here."

He turned and went back into the club. Zarah got home around 10:00pm to a note from David on her door and voice mail messages from him waiting for her. But she was too absorbed in her fear to care, let alone call back as he had asked. She climbed into a hot water bath with lots of lather and cried until she was sleepy. The ringing of the phone continued into Sunday morning but she ignored it lying there in bed planning and re-planning, angry at herself until she heard banging on her door and her name shouted through. She rose slowly and taking her time, she went and opened the door to an exasperated David.

"Where have you been?"

"Go away." Zarah said and turned to go when David grabbed her hand and turned her back but recoiled at murderous look on her face and let go of her arm. Her eyes were icy jet black slits, and her voice was laced with acidic bitterness. Shocked, he wondered what had changed. He'd thought she was long past this phase.

"Zarah, what is wrong? Please tell me, let me help." He begged with urgency.

"Leave me alone and get lost." Zarah said in an almost unrecognizable voice before falling into her sofa face down.

"Zarah, Z…"

She turned and grabbed the center piece on her table and threw it at him, though she missed.

"Okay, I get it. I'll leave now. I will check on you later."

David left, thinking to call 911 but thought against it assuming she was just going through a transition. Instead, he offered a prayer for her as Uncle Leo would have done.

David called Heritage Chartered Accounting on Monday noon, asked to speak with Zarah and was connected to her extension, but immediately she heard his voice she hung up. David tried to ignore it, thinking that at least she was at work.

David kept calling her office throughout the week just to know that she turned up for work since she still refused to take his calls at her home or on her cell.

It was Sunday; David was getting ready for church service and was thinking that it had been a whole week since he saw Zarah or spoke to her. Thoughts of what could have gone wrong were beginning to drive him crazy. He wondered if it was a bad idea to bring her out of Yukon. It was just a month yet things seemed worse than anything he could have imagined. His cell phone rang.

"Where are you?"

"Who is this?"

"Tom. Are you with Zarah?"

"No…"

"Do you know where she is? When did you see her last?" Tom asked, tripping over his words and out of breath.

"I haven't seen her nor talked to her in a week. She refused to …."

"She is on her way to LA and she's got a gun." Tom said still out of breath.

"What?" David screamed, panicked at the thought of what that might mean.

"How did…?"

"Lemon said she came around yesterday night and bought a gun saying something about needing to settle something once and for all back at home."

"Who is Lemon and why is he selling a gun to her?"

"David just get the hell after her. I will kill Lemon myself." The line went dead.

David blanked out for a second with confusion. He felt drained of all energy. Regaining himself he called the travel agent he often used, who told him the next flight to LA was in 3 hours.

"Thank you Jesus." He muttered.

Enough time to put things together and get to the airport.

Madison, who had moved back into Sam's house on the instance of Donald and Associates, was going into her room as she came in from her church service when she heard a loud crashing sound in the library. She turned and went in that direction. Opening the door, she peeked in and asked if anyone was there.

"Yeah, come on in. It's about time you joined me."

"Zarah!" She shouted in surprise but was stopped short as she saw the gun in Zarah's hand aimed at her.

"What is this Zarah, what are you doing? How did you come in?" Madison asked confused and filled with fear.

"This is my house too, as I recall. Madison, come on in and take a seat."

Zarah was so different from what Madison could remember. She was now a woman, but with cold, dark, hate-filled eyes. They glittered as glazed with diamond dust. What had gone wrong with Zarah? Where had she come from and why would she want to kill her?

She moved into the room and took the nearest seat, "Zarah please put away the gun and tell me what the problem is."

"Ha ha… like I had ever listened to you."

"Fine, but what is the problem, why would you have gun aimed at me?"

"Don't play innocent with me Madison."

"Honestly I do not know."

"For starters, you robbed me of my degree certificate?"

"How would that be?"

"Yes, how would that be Madison? You refused to pay my school fees in my last year because you wanted to make sure I didn't get to write my professional exams and take over Harrison Inc."

"Is that what this is all about?" Madison asked in a broken whisper.

"Yes. I even came to you but you shooed me off like a fly."

"Zarah, Zarah…' Madison cried. 'I never intended any evil toward you."

"You never huh? But you killed him, my dad, and your husband."

"No!" Madison cried out. Making gestures with her hands, she moved to get up as if to emphasis her point.

"Sit or I will shoot you."

Madison broke down and cried, covering her face with her hands.

"No, I didn't kill Sam. He died of a heart attack."

"So they said"

Ignoring her, Madison continued.

"Sam had been hypertensive for a while. He had his medicines but stopped taking them a few months before the attack because he thought he had brought it under control."

"Liar! He would have told me, he told me everything."

"He didn't want to upset you with his health issues. Check his medical file, it's all there."

"Shut up! Shut up or I shut you up."

Madison cried harder.

"You may not have killed him but you had your plan on how to make everything yours."

"Nothing is mine, only what was given to me which was Better Homes."

"Yeah right, nothing is yours but you are now CEO of Harrison Inc. and you live here. How very convenient."

"Zarah, I just took over Harrison Inc. and moved in here three months ago. I never wanted anything of yours but you just got up and left. I only felt it was time someone in the family took care of things."

"Now tell me Madison, tell me how it happened that after Dad's death, all of a sudden I didn't have any money paid into my savings account and even when I came to you, you refused to help me."

"If you only knew how I have regretted that day. I was confused. I was afraid. I thought you came to me only to mock me. Oh Zarah, I am so sorry." She cried.

"Shut up and stop calling my name you wicked Russian woman."

Madison cried even harder, not comprehending the vendetta she felt oozing from every single word Zarah spoke.

"And the money equally stopped coming because of your fear too?"

David chose that moment to run into the library but stopped short on seeing Zarah with a gun aimed at Madison.

"Zarah! What are you doing? Put that gun down!' David shouted, fear straining his voice.

"Stand back or I shoot, nobody invited you."

Turning to Madison, Zarah shouted "Answer me!"

"I never knew Sam had a daughter when I agreed to marry him. He….."

"Spare me the tale."

Ignoring her, Madison continued.

"Sam assured me that I never needed to worry about you, that he would make sure you were taken care of and he made it clear what I was entitled to and what you were entitled to. He gifted me with Better Homes but never told me that he had your savings account linked to it. So when I sold Better Homes, naturally all links to it were broken. I didn't find out until recently how it had affected you. Oh Zarah I'm so sorry, I never meant to hurt you. I love you so much just like I loved your father."

"Shut Up!"

Zarah practically went wild with screaming as she broke into tears but somehow, she managed to keep the gun trained on Madison, threatening to shoot.

David realized for the first time the demons Zarah had been fighting and knew that she had reached a breaking point; he saw how easily things could go wrong and quickly came up with a plan.

As Zarah told Madison how she had suffered untold hardship in the past few years while she, Madison, lived off her father's wealth, told her how her plan to murder Madison had been the only thing to keep her going and told her no amount of pleading or excuses would stop her, David tried again to intervene.

"Zarah please do not do this, there are other ways to resolve this. Please put the gun down before you hurt someone."

"Shut up! I will kill her and kill myself."

"No! Zarah please.., Don't! Please. I love you Zarah. Don't do this."

"Shut up, shut up." Zarah cried out.

She felt panicked, with so many varying emotions warring inside her; the hatred she had been harboring all these years, regret that she had wasted all that time for nothing, pity for what Madison herself must have gone through and love, new and nearly overwhelming. Love! The word she had longed to hear, the emotion she'd longed to experience for years until she'd despaired of ever finding it and had given up. She cried hard and buckled, lowering the gun. David, sensing his moment, took a step toward her but she snapped her head up and shot through her tear blinded gaze.

"No!" Both David and Madison cried.

EPILOGUE

Tom pulled up in front of Uncle Leo's farm house just as Uncle Leo was rounding the corner. He stepped out to greet Uncle Leo but worried that he had got lost.

"Hello old Leo." Tom said stretching out his hand for a hand shake.

"Hello Tom." Shaking Tom's hand. "How are you doing?"

"Great, I'm sorry I didn't know this was your place. I came out here to see a Mrs. Duke, but I guess I'm lost"

"Oh no, you are at the right place. Please follow me." Winking at Tom, he turned to walk back to the house."

"He is here." Uncle Leo called into the house as they entered. First to come waddling down was Chuzzy who walked passed Tom to sit by the door. Then, came Zarah looking more radiant than he had ever seen her. Tom would not have recognized her on the street. The clothes, her hair and overall disposition, she looks the part of the heiress David said she was but what was she doing here? David was close behind her and then a slightly older woman he didn't know. What was going on?

"Hello Zarah, David." Tom nodded towards Madison.

"Hello." All three echoed in unison.

"Good to see you again Tom." Zarah said.

"Me too." He nodded again, "I'm here to see a Mrs. Duke?" Tom said looking at Madison.

"I am Mrs. Duke," Zarah said.

"I …. David Duke?"

"Yep, that's right." David said.

"Like hell, I should have known."

They all laughed.

"Please sit down Tom." Zarah said.

"Thank you." Tom said still looking at them in wonder.

"I called you because I have acquired The Stone Family Restaurant."

"You are the one who bought it?"

"Hmm." Zarah nodded.

"Great. So, are you firing us?"

"Why should I? You, my dear Tom, are now a part-owner; owning a 15% share,"

"How is that?" Tom asked awe struck.

"Consider it a payback, Tom. Thanks for all your help. David told me you never cashed his check for that weekend. Not that I have forgiven you for trading me but thanks all the same."

"I'm speechless."

They smiled as Zarah continued.

"I will be making some changes."

"Like? Fire people?"

"Maybe but I wouldn't start with that. First we are changing the name to "Sam's," I will do a total remodeling and re-hire anyone who wants to come back under a new contract. I would like for them to know who bought over the restaurant before they sign on and you my dear Tom, we have got papers to sign so you can take possession of your share."

Tom couldn't say a word, he just blindly stared from one to another.

"How is Lemon?" David asked.

"Mending up, I believe…"

"What did you do to him?"

"Nothing that he didn't deserve." He eyed Zarah.

"You rogue!"

"I would have done same to you if you were in his place."

"Before I forget." Zarah said interrupting the two men. "The Emoss club building is part of the deal. It will be converted into a bed and breakfast and go by the name 'Maddy's Inn'. That, you will supervise and please find something worthwhile for Lemon to do there if he agrees."

"That swine!"

"He was nice to me." Zarah smiled, then rose and went through the sliding glass doors to the back deck.

Standing on the back deck and leaning on one of the beams, David turned as Zarah came out.

"You did it my Darling!"

"No you did it. I am glad I missed that shot that hopeless day. Thanks to you and your confession." Zarah said walking into his arms, out stretched to engulf her in a sweet, warm embrace, kissing her intimately. When he let up and smiled down at her, Zarah said;

"Thanks for loving through my twisted nature and bringing out a more amiable me. I love you my darling."

"I love you too darling!"

OTHER BOOKS
BY THE AUTHOR

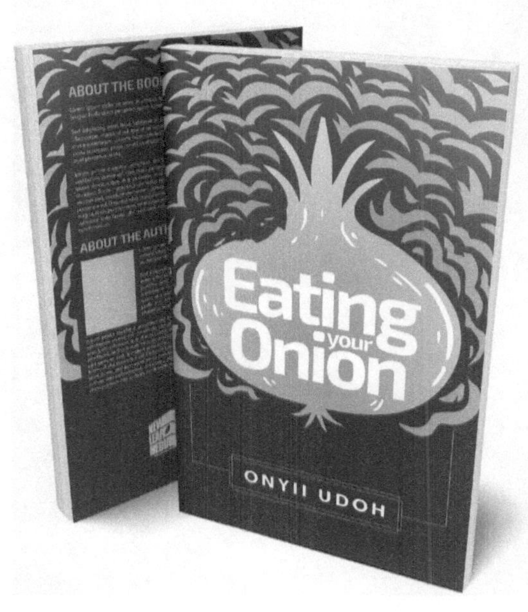

UPCOMING TITLE;

IROEGBUNAM
(MAY HATRED NOT KILL ME)

www.ingramcontent.com/pod-product-compliance
Lightning Source LLC
Chambersburg PA
CBHW030757200726
48288CB00004B/1222